Jade paced back and forth across the cracked cement, unable to go back inside and face her mom yet. How dare her dad judge her mother, the woman who raised her all alone, without any help from him? How dare he think he could just drop back into her life and tear it apart?

Hot tears spilled from her eyes and down her cheeks. She wiped them away, even angrier now that he'd made her cry. Her hands were shaking, and her chest felt tight. Desperate to do something, anything, she banged a fist into the metal doors of the apartment development's mailboxes. Metal shuddered with a sharp, satisfying bang. The contact made her fist tingle.

Jade sank down on the ground and rubbed her red knuckles. Her breath came in short, sharp gasps as she tried to stop crying. Maybe he'd change his mind about filing for custody. He'd get home to his real life and forget all about her again. That could happen, right?

If it didn't, she had absolutely no idea what she was going to do.

Don't miss any of the books in SWEET VALLEY HIGH
SENIOR YEAR, an exciting series from Bantam Books!

Visit the Official Sweet Valley Web Site on the Internet at:

www.sweetvalley.com

Francine Pascal's

SVH senioryear

Too Late

CREATED BY
FRANCINE PASCAL

BANTAM BOOKS
NEW YORK • TORONTO • LONDON • SYDNEY • AUCKLAND

RL: 6, AGES 012 AND UP

TOO LATE

A Bantam Book / February 2001

Produced by 17th Street Productions,
an Alloy Online, Inc. company.
33 West 17th Street
New York, NY 10011.

ISBN: 0-553-49342-6

Visit us on the Web! www.randomhouse.com/teens

Published simultaneously in the United States and Canada

Bantam Books is an imprint of Random House Children's Books, a
division of Random House, Inc. BANTAM BOOKS and the rooster
colophon are registered trademarks of Random House, Inc. Bantam Books,
1540 Broadway, New York, New York 10036.

PRINTED IN THE UNITED STATES OF AMERICA

OPM   0 9 8 7 6 5 4 3 2 1

To Isabella Rose Vaccaro

Jeremy Aames

I know it sounds dopey, but being back together with Jessica just makes me feel like I'm dreaming, all the time. I've always got that fuzzy, happy feeling in the pit of my stomach no matter what I'm doing. All I can think about is when I'll see her again—but even if I'm not with her, everything just floats by around me.

I'm going to stop before I make <u>myself</u> sick.

Ken Matthews

A few months ago every dream I ever had for the future seemed shot down for good. But now I've got my spot back on the team and a chance for a scholarship to a Division I school. I'm even getting along okay with my dad. Suddenly those old dreams don't feel so out of reach anymore.

Jade Wu

Okay, since there's no way my father could actually be standing here in my living room saying that he's suing for custody of me, I'm obviously dreaming. And I'm ready to wake up any time now.

CHAPTER
Self-control

Jade Wu squeezed her eyes shut, willing herself to come out of this nightmare. As if she'd be that lucky. When she opened her eyes, her father was still there, his mouth set in the familiar rigid, disapproving line. And the tension in the small apartment was as thick as it had been two seconds ago when Mr. Wu had uttered those terrifying words.

Jade needs a responsible influence before it's too late. That's why I've decided to sue for custody of our daughter.

She needed *his* influence? Not likely. Jade dug her fingernails into her palms. Why couldn't he just disappear back into his perfect little life back in Oregon and leave her and her mother alone?

Mr. Wu pulled back the sleeve of his brown sport coat and frowned down at his watch. "I have to get to the airport," he said. He glanced over at Jade's mom, who still seemed to be in shock. "Why don't you walk me out?" he asked Jade. He didn't even wait for her to answer him—he just yanked open the front door and walked outside. Jade glared at his back, trying to decide what to do. She wanted to let him go, but now wasn't the best time to make him angry.

Jade looked back at her mother. Ms. Wu sagged against the bookshelf in the small hallway, her hands clenched tightly together. Deep lines were etched around her mouth, and her skin looked pale. She seemed so . . . *small*.

The knot in Jade's stomach grew stronger. Her mother was obviously terrified—which meant she believed this could really happen. He couldn't actually come in and tear their lives apart like this, could he?

Jade took a deep breath and tried to give her mother a reassuring smile, then followed her dad outside.

He was waiting for her next to the fancy Mercedes he'd rented. She stopped about six feet away, feeling the soft grass tickle her toes through the sandals she'd slipped on. She wrapped her arms protectively around her waist and pretended to study the metallic paint on his car.

Mr. Wu sighed. "I know you're pretty old for us to be talking about a custody battle, Jade," he said, "but I think it's important that something about your lifestyle changes—soon."

Jade clenched her teeth together so tightly, her jaw started to ache. *Go away,* she begged silently. *Just go away. Go away, go away, go away.* Tears backed up behind her eyes, making the outline of the Mercedes grow fuzzy.

"I realize you probably don't want to hear this," her father continued, "but your mother's never been a good—"

Jade's body stiffened, and her eyes narrowed into a glare. He could say whatever he wanted about her, but he'd better not start insulting her mom unless he wanted a serious battle.

He must have read her expression because he stopped and started again. "I can see that your mother's not giving you the proper supervision," he said. "You're almost an adult now, and you need stability, or you're never going to develop a sense of responsibility. There's not much time before you're out on your own. I have to believe a judge would listen to me."

Jade bit her lower lip to keep from yelling at him. A judge might listen, but she never would.

"I can see that you're not happy about this," he added, "but as your parent, I need to do what I think is right. Your future is too important."

Jade had to use every ounce of self-control not to lash out at him. *Parent? Since when have you been a*

3

parent? Since you left us alone a million years ago?

She reached up with shaking fingers to push a few strands of black hair away from her eyes and caught her father staring at her stomach.

Damn. She yanked her T-shirt back down, but it was too late. From the way his eyes widened and his mouth turned down, she could tell he'd noticed her belly-button ring.

He opened his mouth to comment, but then quickly shut it and just shook his head. Jade imagined she could hear the thoughts running through his head. *What kind of mother would let her daughter do that?*

Her father just did not get it. The great thing about Jade's mother was that she let her be her own person. Something her uptight father would never stand for.

"I'm sorry I have to leave," he said. "But I'll be back soon. Once I can get things cleared up at work, I'll be down to talk to an attorney and file court papers."

Jade stared down at her feet. She wiggled her toes, watching the sunlight glint off the glitter in her sparkly green toenail polish. If she ignored him long enough, would he just go away?

"Maybe it's best I'm gone for a while," he said. "I can see that you're going to need some time to get used to the idea of living with me and Susan. I don't expect you to know what's good for you, but I think in time you'll see that we have a lot to offer."

Jade watched a yellow-and-black-striped butterfly flit across the lawn. Had she really spent all those years when she was a kid wishing her father would be a part of her life? How dumb was she?

Mr. Wu took a step toward Jade, and she caught a whiff of his spicy aftershave, a scent she remembered from long ago. That was her dad—he never changed anything in his routine.

She winced as he kept coming closer, her shoulders tightening. He was going to hug her. She didn't think she could stand it.

He wrapped an arm awkwardly around her rigid shoulders. Jade didn't move a muscle—she didn't even breathe. Her father sighed and let go of her. He shook his head and tried to smile at her, but the edges of his mouth barely curled up. "This is going to work, Jade. You'll see that soon, I hope."

Jade took a step backward. No, it wasn't going to work. She'd make sure of that.

Her father turned and climbed into his luxury car, and Jade fled back across the courtyard before he got the door closed. From her front door she watched him pull out into the street and disappear around the corner.

Jade paced back and forth across the cracked cement, unable to go back inside and face her mom yet. How dare he judge her mother, the woman who raised her all alone, without any help from him? How dare he think he could just drop back into her life and tear it apart?

Hot tears spilled from her eyes and down her cheeks. She wiped them away, even angrier now that he'd made her cry. Her hands were shaking, and her chest felt tight. Desperate to do something, anything, she banged a fist into the metal doors of the apartment development's mailboxes. Metal shuddered with a sharp, satisfying bang. The contact made her fist tingle.

Jade sank down on the ground and rubbed her red knuckles. Her breath came in short, sharp gasps as she tried to stop crying. Maybe he'd change his mind. He'd get home to his real life and forget all about her again. That could happen, right?

If it didn't, she had absolutely no idea what she was going to do.

"I look like a seventh grader."

Melissa Fox turned sideways and studied her profile in the full-length mirror, then stuck out her tongue. The white dress she'd borrowed from her friend Cherie was all wrong for her—it really did make her look like a little kid. And that was *not* the impression she had in mind for her date with Ken tonight.

Frustrated, she pulled the dress off over her head and dropped it in a heap at the foot of her bed. Getting dressed for a date with Will had never been this hard. She knew him inside and out. But things with Ken were still pretty new. It was tough to guess what he might be thinking, and what he thought at this point mattered. Big time.

She closed her eyes, replaying scenes from Sweet Valley's last football game in her head. A small thrill rippled through her. She'd been out there in front of the whole school, cheering for Ken, the star quarterback, and everybody watching knew they were a couple. The star quarterback and the cheerleader. Just like it was supposed to be.

It was good to be back.

She grabbed a blue sleeveless sweater and her slim black capris out of the closet and held them up to her body. *Perfect.* It was exactly what she needed—an outfit that flattered her slender build and petite body without making her look young. And it was also very different from the way Ken's ex, Maria Slater, dressed. Letting Ken know she was the kind of girlfriend who took the time to look especially good for him would score major points. Hopefully.

7

Melissa stepped into the pants and zipped them up. It bugged her to have to admit it, but Maria Slater had been on her mind a lot lately. She probably didn't have anything to worry about, but when it came to keeping her hold on Ken, probably wasn't good enough.

Ever since the scholarship competition last week, where Melissa and Maria had both been up against each other for the same award, Melissa had been wondering just how over things really were between those two. If Ken hadn't stuck up for Maria so many times during the competition, she wouldn't have been too worried. He'd still been trying to keep her happy, and he'd even made it clear that he'd voted for her in the end. But she wasn't blind—she'd caught those little looks he gave Maria during the student-board interview and the way his eyes were fixed on her the night she won the award.

Melissa pulled on the sweater, then reached for her hairbrush. If she had even the smallest reason to be suspicious, she was going to stay alert. She'd learned that if she didn't watch her back, things could slip away from her way too fast. She dragged the brush through her hair, admiring the way her new shampoo gave the long brown locks extra shine. *Life would be much less complicated if I had a way to know for sure how Ken felt about her,* she thought.

8

She heard the sound of a car engine outside and walked over to her window. Pulling aside the lacy curtain, she saw Ken parking his Trooper by the curb. As she watched, he hopped out of the car and headed across her lawn. He moved like an athlete—strong, confident, and quick.

Like Will used to move. She jerked back from the window. Why was she thinking about Will? Will and Ken were totally different people. Yeah, they were both blond, blue-eyed, and broad shouldered. Ken's hair didn't have that same flop in the front, though, and his clothes weren't as preppy as Will's. Ken was a faded-Levi's-and-T-shirt guy, and she was starting to like that. Ken was a little rougher around the edges, and he had his own mind. He didn't always agree with her the way Will did.

Stop thinking about Will, she ordered herself.

Melissa grabbed her purse, slipped on a pair of black, flat mules, and hurried down the stairs toward the front door. She opened it before Ken reached the top step.

He glanced at her in surprise, then grinned. "Hey," he said softly.

"Hey," Melissa answered.

"So, are you ready?" he asked, shifting from one foot to the other. His gaze moved to something behind her, and he seemed to be looking for someone.

She still hadn't introduced him to her parents. She wasn't sure why.

"Sure," she said, quickly shutting the door behind her. "Let's go."

They strolled toward his car, side by side. When they reached the Trooper, he started to continue around to the driver's side, but then he noticed she'd stopped, and he came back and opened the door for her first. She smiled to herself as she climbed into the passenger seat. Yes, she definitely had to figure out where Maria Slater fit into Ken's life—because she could really fall for a guy like him. He was even beginning to learn the way she needed to be treated. So how could she make sure she knew where things stood?

Melissa pursed her lips, waiting for Ken to get in and start the engine. The obvious idea was to find a way to watch him around Maria—see what he'd do if Maria was around for their date.

And Maria works at First and Ten, Melissa realized. Which meant that she'd suddenly developed a craving for a big, juicy—yuck—hamburger.

She tucked her hair behind her ear and glanced over at Ken. "I was thinking about dinner," she said, "and I'm dying for a burger. How about if we just go to First and Ten?"

He pulled out onto the street, his brow getting

just the slightest furrow. "But I thought we were going to an Italian place," he said. "Didn't you say you wanted seafood?"

Melissa shrugged. "Yeah, I did, earlier. But I changed my mind. That's allowed, right?" she teased. "To think you want one thing for a while and then realize it's all wrong and something else would be much better?"

Ken frowned. "Yeah, um, that's fine," he said, sounding strained. "But First and Ten just isn't—" He paused, coughing. "It just doesn't sound good to me," he said. "How about Chinese?"

Melissa wrinkled her nose. She'd been right—he didn't want to be anywhere near Maria. *Which means that's exactly where we need to go.*

"Okay, no Chinese," Ken said, misunderstanding her expression.

Melissa laughed. "Wow. We're already acting like people who've gone out forever and can't think of what to do."

Ken didn't laugh. He didn't even crack a smile. "So, I guess we should make a decision," he said, gripping the steering wheel tightly. "I need to know where to go," he added, nodding at the traffic light coming up. "How about if we grab a sandwich at House of Java?"

Melissa shook her head. "I'm starving. They just

11

have light things there," she said. "And I really want a burger."

"We could go to Hamburger Heaven," he suggested.

Melissa felt her frustration grow. Was he really *that* desperate to avoid Maria? This was worse than she'd thought. "That's all the way over by Big Mesa," she said. "Besides, their fries are terrible." She stopped, lacing her hands together in her lap. "Is there some other reason you don't want to go to First and Ten?" she asked, staring straight at the road in front of them.

"No, of course not," he said quickly. "I guess if that's what you're really in the mood for . . ." His voice trailed off.

Melissa grinned. "Great, let's go there, then," she said. *Hopefully Maria will be working tonight,* she thought. *And Ken will have one more chance to prove I'm the one he wants.*

Jade scraped the remains of her pork chops into the trash under the kitchen sink and slammed the cupboard door shut. She'd barely been able to do more than nibble at them—her appetite just wasn't there tonight.

A key turned in the front door. Jade glanced at the digital clock on the microwave. She hadn't even realized it was this late already, and her mom would be coming home from her afternoon-evening shift at the bar where she worked part-time.

Jade poked her head around the kitchen doorway to the living room. "Hi, Mom," she said as Ms. Wu walked into the apartment and shut the door behind her. "There's some leftover pork chops and rice in the fridge."

"Thanks," her mother answered, her voice flat. She let her purse slip off her arm onto the bookshelf, then crossed over to the sofa and sank down onto it. "Maybe I'll have some later," she said. "I'm not very hungry right now."

Frowning in concern, Jade followed her mom into the room and sat down next to her. She studied her closely, taking in her pale face and the deep creases around her eyes. She looked exhausted and worn out. As usual. Which was why Jade had been trying harder to cook meals. If she didn't cook, she knew her mother didn't eat. And since she'd ended up in the hospital, Jade had realized just how fragile her mother's health was. "You need to eat something," she insisted.

Her mother kicked off her dark flats and leaned back against the sofa. "I'll get a snack later," she promised, letting her eyes close. "I'm just too tired."

Jade bit her lip. "Mom, are you okay?" she asked. "You didn't even say anything after Dad left—you just ran off to work before we could talk."

Her mother opened her eyes again and met Jade's gaze. "There are so many things I could have done differently," she said softly, shaking her head. "Why didn't I finish getting my degree when I had the chance? I'd have a better job now, and we'd be able to—"

"Mom, you've done a great job. You have." Jade balled her hands into fists. A thick lump filled her throat. This was all her fault. If she hadn't let it slip to her dad during his brief visit that her mom had been sick, if she'd acted more like a perfect child, if she hadn't let her friend Mike stay over last night . . . her father would have just taken off back to Oregon without giving her a second thought. But now, because of her, he thought her mother was a mess, and he had the perfect excuse to put her through even more than he had in the past.

"Thanks, sweetie," Ms. Wu said, flashing Jade a weak smile that didn't quite reach her eyes. "But maybe you *would* be better off with your father. He's got money and—"

"Don't say that," Jade interrupted. Anger boiled over inside her, pushing away the guilt and fear. "He's not even a father. He's a stranger. You're the one who's always taken care of me." She shook her head. "The most he does is send me a birthday card every year. And they're not even from him! Doesn't he think I notice the messages are always written in *Susan's* handwriting?"

Ms. Wu reached up to pull her hair loose from its sleek ponytail, letting the dark strands fall around her face. "Are you saying you don't want to go with him?" she asked.

"Are you kidding? Of course I don't," Jade answered. "It's not even a question."

"You're sure?" her mother pressed. "Because I don't want you to worry about my feelings. I want you to do what's best for you."

Jade smiled. "Being with you is what's best for me," she said.

Finally Ms. Wu's lips curled up into a genuine smile, easing the tension in Jade's chest. "We make a pretty good team, don't we?" she asked Jade.

Jade nodded, but the words only made her feel worse. They would be a good team if she hadn't messed things up so badly.

Jessica Wakefield

English literature short-essay question: Do you think that Pip, the protagonist in Charles Dickens's *Great Expectations*, and Estella deserved to find true love at the end of the story? Why or why not?

Yes, Pip deserved to be with Estella in the end. Both of them had suffered and learned to be better people — especially Estella. It was partly Miss Havisham's fault they didn't get together sooner because of the way she had raised Estella. It was also bad timing. Just when Pip was going to come back and see her, she was getting ready to marry someone else. Then they had to wait years until Estella's husband died.

I know a lot about bad timing. And I bet once Pip and Estella finally got a chance to be together, they wouldn't let anything else stand in the way.

CHAPTER
Quicksand
2

Stop staring, Jeremy Aames commanded himself for the hundredth time since the waiter had placed their dinner in front of them. He averted his gaze from Jessica's face for a second, then immediately glanced back. How could he *not* stare? She looked amazing.

The lighting in the restaurant was dim, but he could have sworn she was blushing. Jeremy twisted the paper napkin in his lap. He just couldn't seem to get it through his head that he and Jessica were back together, even though it had been a couple of days now.

Jessica stabbed a piece of ravioli with her fork. "I'm so glad the new Jackie Chan movie's playing downtown," she said. "I can't wait to see it."

Jeremy nodded. She was gorgeous, *and* she liked Jackie Chan. Girls just didn't get much better.

Their waiter appeared by the table, seemingly from nowhere, the way waiters always did in this kind of restaurant. He clasped his hands behind his back. "Is everything okay here?" he asked.

Jeremy grinned. He couldn't help it. "Everything's perfect," he answered. The spaghetti, being back with Jessica, the salad, being back with Jessica . . .

Jessica caught Jeremy's eye and laughed. "I think we're fine," she told the waiter.

Right as the waiter was walking away, Jeremy noticed another waitress carrying a towering piece of chocolate cake as she passed by.

Jessica leaned over the table toward Jeremy, the candlelight flickering over her blond hair. "I think we need one of those," she whispered.

Jeremy smiled. "Just what I was thinking," he said. They really were on the same wavelength. He took a sip of water, then cleared his throat. "So, hey, I heard our cheerleading squad lost to El Carro last week at the competition," he said. "That's good news for you guys, isn't it?"

Jessica nodded. "Yeah, it is," she replied. "We've definitely won our division now."

Jeremy dragged his fork through the spaghetti, debating if his stomach could take any more of the pasta and still fit dessert. "So your squad is going to regionals, then, right?" he asked, dropping the fork down on the plate.

"Yeah," Jessica answered. She frowned, and her blue-green eyes lost a little of their spark.

"Why aren't you more excited?" he asked, confused.

He knew cheerleading meant a lot to her.

Jessica bit her lower lip and shook her head. "I am excited," she explained. "I'm just annoyed about what they're doing to this girl on my team, Annie Whitman. Coach Laufeld said Annie might not get to go to the Santa Barbara competition with us. I can't believe that. It's not fair at all." Her voice was steadily rising, and she was waving her fork in the air. When she realized it, she placed the fork back down on the table, then folded her arms. "Annie's a junior," she continued, "and she's been on the squad a year already. She's one of our best cheerleaders, and she works *so* hard."

Jeremy nodded. "So why won't your coach let her go?" he asked, reaching over to break off one last small hunk of bread.

"Oh, she has this stupid rule that if you miss three football games, you aren't eligible for squad competitions," Jessica said, rolling her eyes. "Isn't that ridiculous?"

Jeremy blinked. "Uh, actually, that sounds pretty clear-cut," he said. "If she missed the games . . ."

"But Annie's the best flyer we have," Jessica argued. "And she's worked really hard on her jumps."

"Okay," Jeremy said. "That's great. But she still missed three games where the rest of you probably needed her."

Jessica's head jerked back slightly. "She had good reasons, though," she said. "One time her mom made her go on a trip to see her grandparents. It's not like that was her fault." Jessica paused, her gaze fixed on him. "Some of us are thinking about protesting and telling the coach we won't go either unless she changes her mind. She can't go with half a squad."

Jeremy couldn't believe what he was hearing. "Are you sure you want to do that?" he asked.

Jessica's eyes narrowed. "Why not? Don't you think it's more important to stick up for your friends than to win some competition?"

"But Jess, she broke the rules," he protested. "It's not like your coach is picking on her for no reason. Besides, what about having some loyalty to the rest of your squad? You're going to ruin everyone's chances?"

Jessica pushed away her plate and leaned back in her chair. Jeremy could see her jaw tighten. *Uh-oh.* He'd definitely pushed a bad button.

"I didn't realize you were so *concerned* about Melissa Fox and her little friends," she snapped. He winced. It was worse than he'd thought. "You really think we should just ignore what Coach Laufeld's doing to Annie?" she demanded.

Great, what was he supposed to say now? Jeremy took a huge gulp of water. It was too late to back down. Besides, he really didn't think she was being very mature about all of this. He put down his glass. "Yeah, I do. She knew the rules when she signed up. If your coach makes an exception for her, where does it stop?"

"Well, it's pretty obvious Annie isn't just some slacker."

"And so it's okay for Annie to get special treatment? People can't go around changing the rules just because they don't like them."

Jessica pressed her lips together. "When did you become Mr. Rigid?"

Jeremy sighed and rubbed his hand through his short hair. "I'm just saying . . ." His voice trailed off. *I'm just saying you're wrong—people should live up to their commitments,* he finished silently.

Jeremy watched the flame flickering in the red glass candleholder. The atmosphere at the table had definitely chilled. He glanced at Jessica. She was sitting up very straight in her chair, and her arms were folded tightly over her chest.

Jeremy speared more spaghetti onto his fork and stuck it in his mouth, even though he was stuffed. He chewed slowly. As long as he was eating, he couldn't say something else that would ruin the mood even more. Across the table Jessica was tearing apart a piece of bread and sopping up cream sauce from her plate. She looked up, and their eyes locked.

He tossed back the last swallow of water in his glass and chewed on a mouthful of ice. "Maybe we should talk about something else," he suggested.

Jessica's shoulders relaxed. "Yeah, maybe," she agreed.

Jeremy cleared his throat. "You remember that guy on my football team, Sean Morgan? You met him at one of our games."

Jessica pulled the bread basket toward her. "Tall, curly-haired guy, looks like a weight lifter?" she said.

He nodded. "Yeah, he had that nice girlfriend, Amy."

"Alyssa," Jeremy corrected her.

"Right. Alyssa. Didn't they break up, though?"

"They did, but they just got back together," Jeremy said. Sean and Alyssa were one of the "it" couples at Big Mesa. They'd been dating since junior high. When they broke up, nobody could believe it.

Jessica took the last piece of bread and started slowly buttering it. "That's too bad," she said.

Jeremy frowned. Wasn't getting back together a *good* thing? "What do you mean, too bad?" he asked.

Jessica put down the bread and looked up at him. "Well, Sean obviously couldn't make up his mind about who he wanted to date. Didn't he go out with one of her friends while they were broken up? Why should she get back together with a loser like that?"

Jeremy stiffened. "Alyssa's the reason they broke

up in the first place," he fired back. "She was into Dan Epstein. Sean had the right to do whatever he wanted after that."

"Wait a second—are you saying that just because she made one mistake, he can be a jerk and it doesn't matter?"

Jeremy shifted uncomfortably. He stared at his empty water glass, wondering why no one had come by to refill it. His throat suddenly felt very dry.

Jessica leaned forward across the table. "What are you really getting at?" she asked.

Jeremy let out a nervous laugh. "Getting at? I—I'm just talking about Sean and Alyssa here," he said.

"Right." Jessica nodded.

Jeremy cleared his throat, wondering how things had gotten so tense, so fast. He felt like he was standing in quicksand. One wrong word and he was sunk. But wasn't Jessica taking things a little too personally?

"Um, I don't think I really want dessert any-more," Jessica said, breaking the silence. "I'm pretty full."

"Yeah, me too," Jeremy agreed. He glanced down at his watch. "Hey, we'd better get going anyway if we want to make the movie." He held out his wrist awkwardly.

Jessica twisted her head and squinted at his watch. "Yeah, wow, we'd better hurry," she said, then shot up from the chair.

Jeremy shoved back his own chair and jumped to his feet. He pulled his wallet out of his back pocket. "Let's just pay up front."

"Sure, yeah," Jessica said, sounding as relieved as he felt.

Jeremy followed right behind her as they headed toward the front of the restaurant. After he'd paid for their dinner, they hurried toward the exit. He held open the door for her and then let his hand settle on the small of her back as they walked together to his car. Her skin felt warm beneath the soft fabric of her dress, and he eased his arm all the way around her. She turned and smiled up at him, and instantly the tiny little flicker of panic he'd felt inside the restaurant evaporated. There wasn't anything to worry about. He and Jessica couldn't agree on everything—and part of what he liked so much about her was her strong spirit.

Jeremy sighed, enjoying the feel of the light breeze against his face. This night still had a lot of potential. They'd go to the movie, have a good time, and then . . . well, they could see where things went from there.

*   *   *

Ken didn't even react when the waitress placed an avocado-bacon burger in front of him instead of the Swiss-and-mushroom burger he'd ordered. He was too busy scanning the restaurant, waiting for Maria to pop up from somewhere and worrying about what she'd think when she saw him here with Melissa. It was a total slap in the face—he knew it. And he knew she'd take it as one.

Please let Maria not be working tonight, he thought for the millionth time.

He gave his head a little shake, then reached for the ketchup. Did ketchup even go with avocado? It didn't matter. He wanted to look normal, do what normal guys did on dates. He *was* here with Melissa, and he really should pay attention to her. As he poured the ketchup over his burger, he forced himself to tune in to whatever she had been babbling about since the waitress walked away.

". . . and so Coach Laufeld told Annie Whitman she can't come to the Santa Barbara competition," Melissa said.

Ken nodded, trying his best to seem interested. He flicked his gaze behind her for a second, at the back of the restaurant. A tall, slim figure in a black-and-white-striped referee's shirt backed out of the kitchen doors, balancing a loaded tray on her shoulder. Ken's fingers bit into the tabletop. Then as she

27

turned around, he relaxed and dropped his hands into his lap. *Not Maria.*

". . . thinks it's not fair, but I don't see why. I mean, she missed three games. Those are the rules. But of course Jessica is . . ."

Ken took a bite of his burger, then let his gaze wander again, his heart pounding like crazy. It wasn't like he hadn't seen Maria plenty of times in school since their breakup. During the scholarship competition she'd even been around him and Melissa together. But this was . . . different.

Suddenly the food he was trying to swallow lodged in his throat. The waitress had her back to him—she was handing a basket of fries to a customer on the other side of the restaurant. But this time he knew it was her. He recognized the slope of her long, dark neck and the way her hair curled up slightly around her ears.

Ken picked up his drink and took a long sip, hoping Melissa hadn't noticed him noticing Maria. Melissa had made it clear how angry she could get if she thought he was focusing on his ex. Which he wasn't anyway. It was just an uncomfortable situation. Why had Melissa been so determined to come here tonight? It didn't even seem like her kind of place. If he didn't know better, he'd think she was actually *trying* to make things awkward, to . . .

Ken placed the soda back on the table, hard. He wasn't going to let himself think like that. Melissa was a sweet girl who'd been totally supportive of him during a really major time in his life. He was just being paranoid.

Melissa tilted her head so that her long, dark hair fell across her shoulder. It seemed even shinier than usual as the light from above their table hit a few strands. She smiled at him. "Having fun?" she asked.

Ken forced a smile. "Sure. Great burgers," he said, taking another bite of his. He glanced at Melissa's plate, noticing that she hadn't eaten much of hers. What happened to her huge craving for red meat?

She just hasn't had time to eat much since she's been talking nonstop, he realized.

He risked a quick glance back to where Maria had been a second ago. She was walking away from the table, back toward the kitchen—toward them. Ken froze, hoping she just wouldn't look their way. But right before she pushed open the doors to the kitchen, she looked over in his direction. Her eyebrows shot up, and she stood there, one step away from the doors. Slowly her expression changed from shock to anger, and her brown eyes blazed back at him.

He felt a blush creep up his neck and broke his gaze away, staring down at his plate. When he raised his eyes, he was careful to keep them directed only at Melissa. She swirled a french fry through a puddle of ketchup, watching him quietly.

"We're thinking about getting new uniforms for Santa Barbara," she finally said. "I wanted to go with this sweater that has red on top in this kind of V shape, but Jessica Wakefield and Jade Wu told everybody they think we should get white with red stripes down the arms." She leaned back in her chair, still keeping her gaze locked on his. "I just think that will make us look like football players. Especially girls with, you know, kind of wide shoulders. Like Jessica."

"Huh," he said.

She paused. "You know that new routine we're working on, the one where we do those three cartwheels at the end?"

Ken picked up his knife and started scraping the avocado off his bun. "Uh-huh."

"We're thinking about changing it to two cartwheels and a round off."

"Oh," he said. What else was he supposed to say? Was cheerleading all this girl ever talked about?

Melissa grinned. "Okay, I'll stop now," she said, as if she'd read his mind. She toyed with the silver bracelets on her wrist, reminding him of the way

Maria always used to do that. Maria's bracelets were a little thinner, though, and her wrist was . . .

"So when do you think the fall semester starts at Michigan?" she asked. "I know some schools start in August, but most start in September."

Ken shrugged. "I don't know."

"Well, it's a good idea to find out all the details way in advance. You know, so we can start planning ahead and make sure everything's perfect when we get there."

Behind her the kitchen doors swung open with a bang. Before he could stop himself, his eyes went right in that direction. Maria was backing out of the kitchen, carrying a loaded tray. Ken's gaze followed her tall, lean figure as she headed away from them toward the far corner of the restaurant.

"You know, they haven't offered me the scholarship yet," he told Melissa, shifting in his seat. "It's not a definite thing."

"Oh, you're getting it. Don't even worry about that," Melissa said. "I'm just wondering what the dorms are like there. I hope we can make sure we're in the same building." She dunked a fry in ketchup and held it out toward him. Instinctively he pulled back. Melissa popped the fry in her own mouth and chewed thoughtfully. "Do you think we can request the same dorm?" she asked. "It would really be annoying if we

31

ended up far apart. They have a huge campus."

Ken's stomach lurched. They'd barely been a couple for long, and Melissa made it sound like they were practically married. His hamburger was only half eaten, but Ken pushed away his plate, his appetite killed.

Again he let his stare drift behind Melissa until he'd located Maria. He watched her gracefully balance the tray as she distributed the plates on it to everyone at the table.

A strange, guilty tension filled his chest. It didn't make sense—he and Maria were old news. So why did he feel like he was cheating somehow, being here with Melissa?

Suddenly Melissa straightened and moved around in her seat, twisting her neck to get a perfectly clear view of where his attention was focused. Ken winced. He was in trouble now.

Melissa turned back to face him, and he held his breath as he waited for her response. She ran a finger back and forth along the beaded choker on her neck, a slight smile lifting the corners of her mouth. Ken couldn't tell what she was thinking, but at least she hadn't exploded. That was a good sign, wasn't it?

The truth was, he wasn't really sure what anything meant anymore.

*   *   *

Jade inched open her mother's bedroom door, careful not to make any noise. She stuck her head inside the crack and eyed the figure curled up in the middle of the bed. Her mother was sound asleep. Good.

It seemed like it had taken her mother forever to fall asleep tonight, and Jade was dying to get out. She'd been desperately in need of a trip to the Riot ever since her father had left this morning. It was the only way to escape all the thoughts running around in her head—the combination of the loud music and crowded dance floor was her favorite medicine.

Jade retreated from her mother's room, slowly closing the door again. She grabbed her purse from the living-room couch, slipped her car keys into the back pocket of her embroidered jeans, and then headed for the front door.

Twenty minutes later she was in the middle of the dance floor at the Riot, letting everything go. Her body moved to the beat of the hip-hop song playing, and she grinned at the cute college guy dancing across from her. She'd already worked up a sweat—and she was definitely on the road to forgetting all about daddy dearest.

The song ended, and the guy waved to her. "I'd better go find my friends," he told her. Like her, he was breathing a little hard from dancing. "Maybe I'll catch up with you later."

Jade smiled. "Maybe," she replied, letting her voice take on a playful tone. No doubt—the old party girl Jade Wu was on her way back. She'd been a little sidetracked with the whole Jeremy Aames mistake, but that was in the past.

The guy disappeared into the crowd as another fast song began blaring around them. Jade tucked a damp strand of hair behind her ear. She'd been right—this was just what she needed. A night of dancing to blow all the stupid, stressful thoughts out of her head.

"Hey, wanna dance?" a voice behind her asked.

Jade turned around to see a tall, beefy guy standing with his hands behind his back. From the dark beard stubble and the lines around his eyes, Jade guessed he was more than a couple of years older than she was. His button-down shirt was stretched tight across his stomach. Not her type, definitely, but she was there to dance, not check out potential dates.

"Sure," Jade answered him with a smile.

The guy held out his hand, pointing toward the center of the dance floor. "I'm Brad," he said close to her ear as he followed her through the moving bodies to a clear spot.

"Jade," she answered, her voice raised over the music.

By then they were so close to the DJ, Jade could feel the drumbeat in the soles of her shoes. She moved to the music, letting the waves of sound fill her head. Across from her Brad bounced awkwardly. She winced. The guy had no rhythm. He was also staring at her with a kind of intense gaze. She glanced away, then looked back—and his eyes hadn't left her face.

Just when she was starting to feel seriously creeped out, the music stopped. People shoved their way around her, jostling her as they moved off and onto the dance floor.

Brad took a step closer. "Let's do another song," he suggested.

Something about this guy told her she'd be better off dancing by herself. Jade shook her head but smiled to ease the rejection. "Thanks, but I'm going to sit this one out." She turned to head back toward the tables.

But before she could take a step, he grabbed her arm above the elbow and yanked her around to face him. "One more song," he insisted, pulling her toward him.

"No," she said sharply, tugging back.

His fingers tightened painfully on her skin. He dragged her forward even closer. "Yeah, I think so."

Jade flinched. *Beer breath. Bad beer breath.* She looked up into his face, getting her first clear view of his eyes. When she saw the slightly unfocused glaze in them, her heart started to pound. *Great.* A drunk, obnoxious older guy. Not what she needed tonight.

She pulled against his grip, but it didn't seem to be loosening. "Let go," she insisted.

Brad shook his head and yanked her closer to him. "One more dance," he repeated.

He'd pulled her close enough that she could smell the sweat and the alcohol. Anger and fear sent a spurt of adrenaline through her body. Even though the room was packed, between the pounding music and all the conversations going on nobody had noticed that the guy was giving her a hard time.

Suddenly a large hand gripped Brad's arm just above the wrist and ripped his fingers off her. "She said let go."

Jade whipped her head around. Evan Plummer was standing next to her, his hand wrapped around Brad's wrist. After a second he let go and stepped between Brad and Jade. Evan didn't say another word—he just stared into Brad's unfocused eyes. Brad must have seen something there to scare him off because he finally inched backward. "Whatever," he muttered, then stalked off.

Jade laughed nervously and rubbed her arm.

"Thanks. I didn't want to have to break his fingers," she said.

Evan didn't laugh back. His eyes flicked over her. She was surprised at the level of concern in his gaze. The two of them barely knew each other, but he was acting like she was a good friend of his. Unless he pulled this knight-in-shining-armor bit for any random girl.

He guided her over to the edge of the dance floor, away from the crowd. "Are you okay?" he asked.

Jade shrugged. "I'm fine. It was no big deal," she lied.

"It could have been," he said. He glanced over Jade's shoulder, his mouth set in a tight line. Jade turned and saw Brad shove open the front door and lumber outside.

She took a deep breath and blew it out, willing the shakiness in her legs to go away. Then she hooked her fingers into the belt loops of her jeans and smiled up at Evan. "Thanks, but I've handled guys like that before."

Evan shook his head, his long, dark hair flopping around his face. "I'm sorry there are guys like that," he said, his tone still serious.

Jade cocked her head. "It's not like you're responsible for the whole male race."

"No, but they make guys like me look bad," he said.

Jade grinned. There wasn't much that would make a guy like Evan Plummer look bad. Not only was he gorgeous, but he was smart and funny—and obviously a great watchdog too.

"Can I walk you back to your table?" he offered.

Jade bit her lip. "I'm not really sitting anywhere."

"You're not here with anybody?"

"No." Jade narrowed her eyes. "Are you?"

Evan waved his hand toward a couple of tables beside the bar area where a group of guys sat talking. "I came with some friends from El Carro." He paused. "You come out dancing by yourself a lot?"

Jade lifted her hair up off her sweaty neck. "Sometimes, when I get stressed."

"I guess that makes sense," Evan said. "Exercise can help. I swim when I'm stressed."

Jade let her hair fall back around her face, flashing a smile. "Then you probably don't swim that often," she joked.

"Are you trying to say I'm not in shape?" he challenged, crossing his arms over his chest.

Jade eyed the well-defined muscles in his upper arms and chest. Even through his flannel shirt, she could see he was built. Plus Jessica had filled her in on Evan's secret claim to jockhood as a member of the swim team, so she knew he worked out plenty.

"That's definitely not what I meant," she said.

"It's just—you're such a mellow guy. I can't picture you getting stressed."

Evan laughed. "Well, yeah, I'm into maintaining the positive energies in my life," he said. Jade didn't know a single other person who could say those words with a straight face—and *not* cause her to burst into laughter.

"I guess I just need some positive energies to maintain," Jade muttered.

Evan frowned. "Something pretty big is bugging you tonight, isn't it?" he asked. "Are you okay?"

She tried to smile, but she wasn't sure it worked very well. "You already asked me that," she said softly.

"I don't mean about that jerk from before," Evan said. He pressed his lips together. "You seem like there's something else going on, that's all."

"Well, I'm fine," Jade said, lifting her chin defiantly.

Evan gave a half shrug. "It's cool if you don't want to talk about it," he said. "But you're sending out some major not fine vibes."

"No, I'm—" Jade was cut off as someone's elbow jabbed into her ribs from behind. She turned to glare at the guy, but he and his girlfriend were already making their way through the dance floor.

"This isn't exactly a great place to talk," Evan said. "You want to go somewhere quieter? I could bail out on the rest of the guys, no problem."

She was about to say no, automatically. She wasn't the type to *talk* about her problems—she preferred to sweat them out. But something stopped her. Maybe it was the total sincerity in his bright blue eyes. Maybe it was the idea of going somewhere more private with this very cute, cool guy.

"I guess I could be up for somewhere else," she said casually. She was *not* going to let him think she was desperate to spill her guts.

Evan grinned, showing off his perfectly white teeth. "What about House of Java?" he suggested. "They're open late tonight."

"No," Jade answered right away. She cringed. Why did Evan have to keep seeing her all vulnerable? She didn't want him to know she couldn't deal with seeing the place where her ex-boyfriend worked. "I used to work there," she said. "I could get some strange temptation to start serving people hot beverages."

Evan nodded, his smile widening. "Got it," he said. "There's always that all-night coffee shop down by the highway. The coffee is gross, but it's cheap—and I doubt you'll feel any urges to wait tables there."

"Sounds great," she agreed. She'd set out for an anonymous good time tonight, but a night out with Evan Plummer could possibly end up even better—if she just played things right.

Will Simmons

1. Cut out all sugar.
2. Increase protein intake (maybe three protein shakes a day?).
3. Start lifting at the gym.
4. Stomach crunches. ~~Thirty~~ Fifty a day.
5. As soon as cast is off, run fifteen minutes a day. Increase to thirty minutes a day by week three.
6. Stay psyched. Watch ~~Rocky~~ _Terminator_ and _Die Hard_ for motivation.

CHAPTER
Making Progress
3

Jessica followed Jeremy through the crowded lobby toward the movie-theater exit, letting go of his hand when a big family got in between them.

So we didn't talk during the movie. That's okay, she told herself. *You're not supposed to talk during deeply tragic disaster scenes, right?*

The cool night air hit her as she stepped outside, and she shivered. She searched around for Jeremy, finally spotting him waiting for her on the sidewalk. She quickly wove through the other people to get to him.

When she reached him, he took her hand again, his fingers tightening around hers, and they walked side by side toward his car. As they passed the windows of stores that were already closed for the night, Jessica searched her brain for something to talk about to fill the silence.

A mannequin dressed in fuchsia-and-black leopard-spotted bell-bottoms caught her eye in the window of Boarder Zone. "Wow, that is a major—"

She stopped herself before she could get out the mocking comment, remembering the tense conversation at dinner. What if Jeremy thought spotted bell-bottoms were cute? What if they were, like, his mom's favorite thing to wear at some point and he took her insult really personally? Suddenly she was afraid to say anything to him.

"What did you say?" Jeremy asked.

Jessica just shook her head. "Nothing," she answered.

An older couple walking a tiny white dog was heading toward them, and Jeremy stepped closer to Jessica to let them pass. His shoulder grazed hers, sending familiar waves of warmth through her. Just that small connection made everything feel right. She didn't have to worry about them not having the same opinion on Annie Whitman or a pair of pants—they were together, and they belonged that way.

When they got to Jeremy's Mercedes, he unlocked the passenger-side door first to let her in. She settled into her seat while he stepped around the car and got in the driver's side.

"So that was pretty amazing," he said as he started the engine. "Weren't the special effects great?"

Jessica glanced at his profile in the glow of the streetlight. His eyes glittered with excitement. Her stomach sank. He'd actually *liked* the movie? Aside from watching Jackie Chan fight, she'd been bored to tears.

She twisted the shoulder belt back and forth in her hands. "The effects were okay," she commented.

"Yeah, like those spaceships that came down in the end," he continued, not seeming to notice her lack of enthusiasm. "I wonder if it really would look like that, traveling at light speed." He pulled the car out into traffic, and Jessica stared out the window as Main Street rolled by. What had happened to the mature, sensitive Jeremy she was used to? She never would have expected him to go for a movie with such a lame plot.

"Didn't you think it was kind of, um, sad?" she asked, tugging at the bottom of her dress. "The way all those guys working for Jackie ended up dying? Why couldn't they have figured out how to work the time machine backward?"

"They had to die," Jeremy insisted. "That's what it was all about—they chose to fool around with the laws of physics."

Jessica ground her teeth together. He sounded like he thought she was an idiot for not getting that. "Then why show them being heroic and everything if they were just going to die anyway?" she challenged.

Jeremy cast her a quick glance as he braked for a red light. "I kind of like it that they didn't tie it all up so simply for once, like they normally do so people will be satisfied."

Jessica's cheeks burned. "Are you saying I'm *simple?*" she demanded.

"What? Jess, no. Why are you taking everything so personally?"

Jessica's eyebrows arched up. He was *snapping* at her. Over a movie. "I'm not," she said carefully. "It just really sounded like—"

"Look, all I said was . . ." He stopped, shaking his head. "Never mind. Maybe we should talk about something else." But neither of them said another word until he pulled the car to a stop in front of her house.

Jessica unfastened her seat belt. "Good idea," she agreed, but she couldn't think of anything to say.

They sat in silence, both staring straight ahead through the windshield as the motor idled. A car cruised down the street past them, the headlights washing the inside of the car with bright, harsh light. Jessica could see Jeremy tapping his fingers on the steering wheel. It made her realize her own fingers were knotted together in her lap.

What was happening to them?

Jessica fumbled for the door handle and pushed

open the door. "Call me?" she asked when she was halfway out of the car.

"Uh-huh," Jeremy responded.

She rested a hand on the roof of the car and bent down her head until she could see his face. "Okay, well, thanks," she said.

"Sure." Jeremy's fingers continued to tap on the wheel.

She straightened up and shut the car door.

The motor raced as Jeremy took off down the street. She watched his taillights until they disappeared around the corner, her whole body deflating. Could they really disagree about so many things? How could she never have noticed that before?

". . . so he basically zooms into town after all these years, looks me up, and decides I'm some kind of freak child and he's going to straighten me out," Jade finished, realizing that she'd spilled the whole story in pretty much one breath. She stopped and inhaled deeply.

Evan had been lifting his coffee mug, but at her last statement he put the mug slowly back on the table. "What do you mean, straighten you out?" he asked.

"He *says* he's suing for custody," she explained. She laced her fingers together on the table.

"That is so wrong," Evan declared, his eyes firing up. "This guy's been out of your life all these years and he thinks he can just walk in and take over? Single mothers have rights, you know. This country can't make it easy for someone to take advantage of you and your mother that way."

Jade took a sip of coffee and immediately started drowning the cup in sugar to cut the bitter taste. "He doesn't even know me," she said as she stirred. She cringed, realizing how self-pitying that sounded. What was she doing, pouring out her heart like this? It was turning her into a pathetic whiner.

Evan leaned back against the neon orange booth and folded his arms across his chest.

"Doesn't the guy have any respect for your mother and what she's done for you?"

Jade felt a flash of triumph that Evan got exactly what was wrong with the situation. She wasn't crazy—her dad was out of line, and Evan knew it.

"You'd think," she said. "Except he doesn't really work that way."

Evan reached down and picked up his coffee, taking a sip this time. "Do you think he's serious about the custody thing?" he asked, cradling the mug in his hands.

"I don't know," she responded. Frustrated, she flicked the laminated advertisement for an enormous gazillion-egg breakfast and sent it skidding across the table toward Evan. "With my luck? Yeah. He'll do it."

Evan caught the ad, smiled, and flicked it back in her direction. "Then you and your mom can fight back."

"That's just it—we can't." Jade hesitated, embarrassed to say more. She'd done the sob fest enough tonight. But somehow Evan's gently prodding expression was drawing words out of her almost against her will. "We don't really have a lot of money," she blurted out. "My mom already works two jobs." Panic welled up inside her, squeezing her chest until it was hard to breathe. "What if he wins?" she whispered.

Evan frowned. "We won't let that happen," he assured her.

She blinked, surprised. They weren't exactly a "we," just two people who both happened to be friends with Jessica Wakefield. And maybe they were becoming friends, sort of, on their own. But still—*we?* She tried to ignore the weird warm feeling in her stomach.

"What if you could get some free legal advice?" Evan suggested. "There are people who do that when they believe in your case. We probably even know someone with a parent who's a lawyer." He paused, and then his eyes lit up. "I can't believe we didn't think of it right away—Jessica's dad is a lawyer. I'm sure he wouldn't mind at least talking to you about what to expect, how to prepare for things."

Jade's shoulders sagged with relief. "I forgot all about Mr. Wakefield. You're right; I bet he would talk to me. That's a great idea." She smiled. "Thanks."

"Not a problem." He tilted his half-full cup toward him and scrunched up his nose. "I think I've had enough of this coffee, though."

Jade pushed away her mug. "Me too." She grabbed her purse and dug around for the bills she kept loose in there. She was always forgetting to buy a wallet. "It's on me," she told him as she noticed him reach for his back pocket.

"Are you sure?"

She nodded. "I owe you—for all the advice."

He shrugged. "Okay, cool. Thanks."

Score another point, she thought. She liked it that he didn't get all macho and insist on paying for a couple of stupid coffees. "So are you ready to take me back to my car?" she asked.

"Yeah, of course," he said. He slid out of the booth and led the way out.

"So what about you?" Jade asked after they'd been driving for a few minutes.

"What about me?" Evan asked, turning down the radio. The station was set to some quiet, dreamy song anyway.

"I've spent the whole night talking about my pathetic problems," she said. "So what's the deal on you?"

He seemed to be holding back a smile. "What do you want to know?" he asked.

Are you single? she thought, studying his strong jawline. He was gorgeous, sensitive, and apparently happy. She could pretty much guess the answer to that one anyway. Still, she hadn't seen him with any specific girl at school, and he *was* spending his Saturday night with a bunch of guys.

Jade took a scrunchie out of her purse and pulled her hair back into a short ponytail. "I don't know," she said. "Like . . . what do you do for fun besides swimming?"

Evan rested his hand casually on the top of the steering wheel, his eyes focused on the road. "Lots of things. The recycling program at school is a sham. I'm trying to get the administration to work out a better program. And lately things have been getting pretty busy with the international protest to free Tibet." He glanced over at her, his eyes shining with excitement. "The Dalai Lama is coming to California next month, and I'm trying to get a ticket to see him speak in Berkeley. I'd kill to get in."

Jade laughed. "Doesn't sound like you have much extra time on your hands."

"Not usually." He slowed the car and pulled into the Riot's parking lot, stopping next to Jade's black Nissan. "Anything else you're dying to know?" he asked.

Nothing I'm going to ask, Jade thought. She unbuckled her seat belt and turned to face him. "That pretty much covers your *political* life," she teased. "What about your social life? You know, girlfriends . . . stuff like that," she added quickly. "Or don't you granola boys date?"

Evan chuckled. "We do, but I'm kind of out of that game right now," he said.

Jade raised her eyebrows. "Why's that?" she asked.

He reached forward and played with the keys dangling from the steering column. "Let's just say I've dated one too many rebound girls lately," he said. "I'm taking a little break from relationships."

"Really? A break?" Evan Plummer was getting more interesting by the second. He rescued her and volunteered to listen to her problems, and he wasn't even interested in getting anything back. "I think you're smart," she said. "People jump into things too fast when it's not what they really want." She paused. "Jeremy was kind of on the rebound too when I met him. You're right—it's no fun." She cracked open her door. "Thanks for the ride. And for listening."

"Anytime," he said. He actually seemed to mean it.

"Great." She pushed the door wide. "I can be a pretty good listener too, if you ever need it."

Evan nodded. "I bet you are. I'll remember that." She climbed out of the car and gave him a last wave before shutting the door.

"I'll hang out until you take off," he said, pointing at her car.

Jade pulled her keys out of her pocket. "Thanks—again." Of course he would. Mr. Thoughtful. Mr. Sensitive. Mr. Single.

Mr. Friend, she reminded herself.

She quickly unlocked her car, got in, and started the engine. She pulled out and turned around to head for the exit, and Evan followed her. What a weird night. The stress that had seemed inescapable just a few hours earlier now felt under control. And it was all because of Evan Plummer.

Eighteen . . . nineteen . . . twenty . . . Will groaned and flopped back down on the floor of the family room. His stomach muscles were already quivering, and he had eighty more crunches to go. At least. But that was okay. He was so excited about his last physical-therapy session, he didn't care if he had to do four thousand sit-ups. The therapist had told him he was making great progress, and he knew what that meant—he was going to prove his surgeon wrong. He was going to play football again.

"Yes!" he yelled at the ceiling, and pumped both his fists in the air.

A sharp rap at the front door startled him, making him sit up. He tried to scramble to his feet, but with his cast he had to roll on his side first.

"I'm coming," Will yelled down the hall. He finally made it to his feet and hobbled toward the living room.

"Took you long enough," Matt Wells said the instant Will yanked opened the front door.

Josh Radinsky shoved Matt aside. "Yeah, what's the deal?" he said. "You avoiding us?"

Will hung on to the doorknob for balance and grinned at his friends. "What's up?"

"We're heading to the beach," Josh said. "We caught up with a bunch of guys at the Riot, and they're heading over to Crescent Beach for a bonfire. We thought we'd cruise by and see if you were up for it."

Will thought about the long reconditioning list lying on his desk. "I don't know. . . ."

Matt snorted. "Wuss."

Will rolled his eyes. "I've just got stuff to do," he mumbled. He paused, debating if he should give them the news. But he couldn't hold it inside. "I'm working on getting back in shape," he announced. "The physical therapist says I'm doing great—so

I'm gonna get back out there, on the field."

"That's great, man," Matt said, giving him a light punch on the shoulder.

"No way." Josh held up his hand for a high five, and Will slapped it, barely holding himself up without the added support of both hands.

"I think we need to ce-le-brate," Josh said.

"Yeah, well, not yet," Will said. "I have a long way to go." He glanced back and forth between his friends. "And I might need your help getting back on the team. Ken Matthews could be a problem."

Matt smirked at Josh, who winked back. "Whatever you need, buddy."

"Totally." Josh nodded. "Ken won't stand a chance once you're back, Simmons."

Will grinned. "Maybe you're right," he said. "Maybe we do need to do some celebrating." He glanced down the hallway at the light spilling out of the family room, where all of his exercise equipment was set up. He could take the rest of the night off, just this once.

He turned carefully and limped back down the hall. He'd grab his crutches and write his parents a note, letting them know where he was. They'd probably get back after he did anyway.

He felt like a million pounds had been lifted off his shoulders. A lot of sweat, some help from the guys, and he'd be back where he deserved to be.

melissa Fox

Ken passed his first test. Yeah, he stared at her. And yeah, it was obvious he wanted to avoid going to where she worked in the first place. But in the end I was the one who got his attention. And I was the one he walked out of there with—not her.

Still, I wish I could feel more certain. It's not like it was with Will. We were together, end of story. Even the whole Jessica Wakefield thing couldn't keep him away long. After tonight, though, I can see Ken moving in the right direction. Before the end of the semester it'll be Kenandmelissa, just like it used to be Willandmelissa.

Well, not exactly. But that's okay. No two relationships are ever the same, right? I can't expect Ken to be Will. And I don't want him to be anyway. Right?

CHAPTER 4

A Whopping Miracle

Jade jolted up in bed on Sunday morning, instantly wide awake. The second her eyes opened, a million unpleasant thoughts crowded her mind. She groaned and turned back over, sticking her pillow over her head. But it was pointless—there was no way she could get back to sleep. With another moan she slid out of bed and padded down the hall. Her mother's door was open, and Jade was surprised to see that she was still asleep. Her mother hardly ever slept later than she did.

Jade tiptoed past her mother's room and into the kitchen. She thought about making some coffee, but she didn't want the noise of the machine to wake up her mom. It was weird that her bedroom door was open—it had been closed when Jade went out last night. Ms. Wu must have gotten up in the middle of the night for some reason.

Like she does when she's worried about something, Jade thought, cringing. She glanced at the clock in the microwave above the stove. Ten-twenty. Not too early to call Jessica.

Jade grabbed the white cordless phone from its cradle and walked back into her room. She shut the door behind her and sat down on the end of her bed, then dialed the Wakefields' number.

"Hello?" It sounded like Jessica, but sometimes Jade had trouble telling her and her twin apart.

"Hi, it's Jade," she said, to be safe.

"Oh, hi, Jade." The disappointment in her tone was obvious, and now Jade could tell it was Jessica— and obviously Jessica had been expecting someone else. "What's up?"

Jade paused, running her hand along her bedspread. She'd been hoping to catch her friend in a better mood. "I have a favor to ask you," she said. "Well, your dad, actually."

"My dad?" Jessica laughed. "Sounds interesting."

"Yeah, I need some legal help. It's about *my* dad. It's pretty crazy, really." She took a deep breath. "He showed up out of the blue last week for this surprise visit, and then he said he's going to try to get custody of me."

"Are you serious?" Jessica said. "But you're seventeen. How can he do that?"

"I know." Jade stared up at the ceiling. "He says he can convince a judge that I need guidance before it's too late. That's why I was wondering if I could talk to your dad. I know I can't let my dad get away with this, and there has to be a way to stop him.

Since your dad's a lawyer, I figured he'd know what to do."

Well, Evan figured, she thought. But somehow she felt weird sharing that part with Jessica.

"Sure," Jessica said quickly. "He handles lots of divorce cases, I think. I bet he would do that. He's out in the backyard. I'll go ask him right now."

"That's great. Thanks."

"Hold on a sec," Jessica said. She put down the phone.

A little while later Jade heard footsteps in the background, and then Jessica got back on the line. "He said no problem if you want to come over this afternoon," she said, slightly out of breath.

Jade grinned. "Sure."

"He told me to warn you that he's superbusy at work, though. He can't take you and your mom on as clients, but he can definitely explain all about the process of filing for custody and what you can expect."

Jade sat up, gripping the phone tightly. "No, that's perfect. That's exactly what I need to know."

"Cool. So come on over, anytime after two, he said."

"Thanks, Jessica."

"Hey, I owe you, remember?" Jessica said, her voice losing some of its enthusiasm.

Jade smiled. "Yeah, you do." That whole getting-Jessica-and-Jeremy-back-together stunt had qualified as her good deed of the year. "But thanks anyway."

Jessica sighed. "Anyway, I'd better get back to this paper I'm working on. I'll see you later."

"Yeah," Jade said. "See you later," she added, then hung up.

She tossed the phone onto the bed, already feeling much better. Mr. Wakefield would explain how all this custody stuff worked, and then she could figure out how to make sure it *didn't* work—for her dad at least.

Jade plumped up the pillows behind her back and grabbed the magazine from her night table, flipping it open. She'd relax and read all about how to find her true love. Then, once her mom woke up, she could tell her the good news—that she'd found a solution to their problem.

"It's third down on the Packers' own twenty-five-yard line with a minute-forty left in the first half," the announcer rattled off from the big-screen television in Ken's living room.

Ken's dad lifted his head off the couch long enough to rearrange the throw pillow under his head. "That guy is going to go exactly nowhere," he said, pointing to the screen. "He couldn't run a fake play option if his butt was on fire."

Ken nodded from the armchair. "No kidding," he agreed.

As they watched, the Packers' quarterback took the snap from the center and threw it wide. It was a wild pass, and it actually landed in a group of cameramen. Ken winced. "Ouch."

"They're definitely gonna lose this one," Mr. Matthews said.

"Probably." Ken glanced over at his father, who was stretched out across the entire couch. The whole scene felt so familiar, in such a weird way. This was how things were between them a long time ago—the two of them watching the games on TV together, commenting on all the plays. No pressure about Ken's own football career. That was before Ken became the star quarterback on his high-school team, then quit, then came back as a second-string player—and then got back on top. Now every game they saw, every conversation they had about the sport, had some extra edge to it. Because Ken knew his dad was wondering if someday that would be Ken out there, throwing passes for an NFL team. And throwing better than the guy on the Packers too.

A car commercial replaced the game, and Ken pushed himself up out of his seat. "I'm gonna get some chips," he said. "You want anything?"

His father crossed his arms behind his head. "I'll take some pretzels," he said.

"Sure," Ken answered. He headed into the kitchen to get the snacks.

When he came back into the living room, a bag and a soda in each hand, the game was back on. His father sat up and took the pretzels and Coke that Ken offered him. "Thanks," he said, then ripped open the bag.

Ken settled back in his chair and ate a handful of chips while the Packers lined up and punted the ball away to the opposing team.

"You hear from that Michigan scout at all this week?" Ken's father asked while the teams were in their huddles.

The chips he'd just put in his mouth suddenly seemed stuck to his gums. Couldn't they spend five minutes together without talking about that?

"Nope," he said in a flat voice. Maybe his dad would get the hint and shut up about Michigan.

"Nothing?" His father's voice rose. "He didn't contact your coach or anything?"

"I don't think so, Dad."

"Huh." Ken heard the pretzel bag crinkle as his father stuck his hand inside. "Practices go okay this week?"

Ken picked at a loose thread sticking out of the arm of his chair. "Practices went great."

"Yeah? You hitting that short rollout any better these days?"

He wasn't, actually. Not even close. His last few practices had been utter disasters. Ken pulled at the thread until the material behind it puckered up. "I'm hitting it," he lied.

"That's good. The scout's gonna want to see you drilling that ball in tight situations. You've got a lot of ground to make up after the beginning of this year, you know."

"I know what he wants to see," Ken muttered. He wound the thread around his index finger and yanked until it broke. *And I know what you want—a star quarterback for a son. A normal, decent guy isn't good enough for Mr. Ace Sports Reporter.*

Mr. Matthews pushed himself up onto one elbow and looked Ken in the eye. "So Riley's happy with how you're throwing?"

Ken's mouth went completely dry. *Uh, not exactly.* Not since he'd fumbled on the ten-yard line yesterday and lost the game. No, he wouldn't say Coach Riley was particularly happy with him. But he wasn't going to give his dad a chance to come down even harder on him. "Coach Riley said I'm working the rollout better than I ever have."

His father grinned and lay back down. "That's my boy." He turned his attention back to the TV.

Right, Ken thought. *I'm yours as long as I'm performing.*

". . . and it's touch do-o-own, Rams," the announcer screamed. Mr. Matthews let out a whoop and thrust his arm up in the air.

Yippee for them, Ken thought. Maybe his father could just adopt the whole damn team and leave him alone.

He got up out of his chair and tossed the open bag of tortilla chips onto the coffee table. "I've got homework," he mumbled, then headed down the hall toward his room.

Jade ran up the steps to the Wakefields' house, catching her breath before ringing the doorbell. The plan had been to finish her homework first and show up at the Wakefields' later in the afternoon, but when it came down to it, she couldn't wait to hear what Mr. Wakefield had to say.

The door swung wide a second after Jade pressed the doorbell button. *Jessica must have seen me driving up,* she realized.

"Hey," Jessica greeted her. Her blond hair was swept back in a messy ponytail, and she had dark bags under her normally bright eyes. Whatever weird mood she'd been in on the phone earlier hadn't seemed to get any better.

"Hi," Jade responded. She stepped inside, and Jessica shut the door behind her. "So, what's up?" Jade asked. She didn't want Jessica to think she didn't care if something was wrong, but she had a feeling whatever it was, she would have trouble mustering up much sympathy. Jessica had the perfect family, the perfect house, even the perfect boyfriend again, thanks to her.

Jessica sighed. "Nothing. I'm just kind of bummed today."

Bummed? As if Jessica had any idea what really being bummed was all about. Jade took in a deep breath and tried to push away the irritation that automatically flared up. Jessica had been a good friend, even when Jade knew she didn't exactly deserve it. She shouldn't be so hard on her.

"Sorry," Jade said lamely.

Jessica shrugged. "I'll live," she said. "Let me tell my dad you're here."

Jessica took off through the kitchen, and an instant later Jade heard her yell out that she was there. Mr. Wakefield followed Jessica back through the dining room. The muddy knees of his faded jeans and the chopped-up bits of grass clinging to the bottoms made it clear he'd spent the whole morning outside. Jade had seen both of Jessica's parents at games before, when they came to watch Jessica cheer. But she'd never actually met Mr. Wakefield.

He smiled at Jade when he saw her. "Hello, Jade," he said. "Come on in my study, and we can talk. Hope you don't mind the casual appearance," he added, gesturing down at his clothes.

Jade smiled. "No problem," she said.

"Come up and get me when you're done," Jessica told her. Then she took off toward the stairs.

Jade followed Mr. Wakefield into his study. The walls of the room were lined with books, and his oak desk was piled high with more books and all kinds of papers. It was a small room compared to the rest of the Wakefields' big, airy home, but it was still bigger than her apartment's living room.

Mr. Wakefield sat down in one of the burgundy leather chairs across from his desk and motioned for Jade to sit in the other one. He sank back in his seat and hitched one ankle across the top of his other knee, then he rested his arms on the rounded arms of the chair. "Okay, now," he said after he'd gotten settled. "What's going on with your father?"

Jade took a deep breath, trying to think how to start. She sat forward on the edge of her seat, her elbows resting on her legs. "My parents were divorced when I was really small," she said. "I haven't ever seen my dad regularly, and in the last couple of years I haven't actually seen him at all. Last week he was in the area for business, and he decided to look me up.

Only he just happened to show up when my mom was at work. I accidentally let him know that she'd been in the hospital a little while ago. He jumped to conclusions and assumed that my mom leaves me alone all the time."

She stopped and glanced up at him. He nodded, a concerned frown on his face. "We don't have a lot of money," she explained. "My mother's almost always had to work two jobs, and she just got exhausted. So my dad decided that because my mother's sick and she's never home, I need more supervision. But she does the best she can," Jade argued.

Mr. Wakefield nodded sympathetically. "I'm sure she does, Jade. I doubt anyone would work two jobs because they wanted to."

"Of course not." Jade smiled back. At least he seemed to understand. Everyone did, except for her dad. Why couldn't he see what was so obvious?

Mr. Wakefield tapped a finger on his chin. "Okay, as far as we know, then, he hasn't actually filed a motion for change of custody." He looked at Jade. "Your mother hasn't been served with any official papers, right?"

"No." Jade sank back in her seat and crossed her arms over her chest. Now he'd tell her how they could get her father off their backs.

Mr. Wakefield sat forward and put his own elbows on his thighs, mirroring Jade's pose. "There's really nothing you and your mother can do until he actually files. That's the good news." He hung his head forward and ran a hand through his hair. Then he lifted his head and looked Jade right in the eye. "Now the bad news. Since your mother has been sick, it sounds like he might be able to convince a judge that she isn't capable of taking care of you right now and—"

"But my mom has to work two jobs," Jade protested. "It's not like she doesn't care about me."

Mr. Wakefield waved a hand in front of him. "I'm not saying she's a bad mother, Jade. And that's not what the courts would say either. What I'm trying to tell you is that your father may be able to make it look like she's not capable of giving you what you need. That's different. Remember, the judge will only get to know what's going on based on the evidence each side presents. He or she won't have a chance to really get to know your mother—or your father, for that matter."

Jade slumped down in her seat. "Great, so if my father makes my mother look like some big loser, he could win?"

Mr. Wakefield ran a hand through his hair again, causing a few strands to stand up on top. Then he nodded reluctantly. "It's a possibility; that's all I'm saying. The important thing is to prove that your mother's health situation will be more stable in the future. And unfortunately, that might not be possible if her work schedule isn't changing."

This isn't happening, Jade thought. A rush of panic washed over her, making her almost light-headed. "But he hasn't even been a parent." Jade dug her fingers into the burgundy leather. "I mean, where was he all these years? He basically abandoned me. Us."

Mr. Wakefield shook his head. He touched the tips of his fingers together. "It's conceivable he could persuade a judge that, for example, because he and your mother fought so much, he thought it was best to stay out of your life. Or he could claim that your mother kept you away from him. I'm not saying he would, but I've seen people do things like that in custody battles."

Jade jerked forward. "But that's a lie!"

Worry lines creased the edges of Mr. Wakefield's eyes. "I'm sure, Jade, but a judge wouldn't know that."

Jade stared down at the carpet, all of her hopes slowly deflating. She'd come here for solutions, not bad news. "So it's whoever makes things look the best, then."

"Sometimes, yes," Mr. Wakefield acknowledged.

"And you're saying my father would look better than my mother?"

"I'm saying that's not out of the question." Mr. Wakefield scanned the bookcase behind Jade's head. "How can I explain this," he muttered. "If he's even thinking about initiating a custody battle, I'm assuming

71

he's got more money than she does, right?"

She snorted. "He's rich," she said.

"And with your mother's work schedule and her health condition . . ." He trailed off. "Jade, I'm not saying this is hopeless at all. You have a very good argument, and it's rare for someone to win custody at such a late time in the child's adolescence. But it's a good idea that you and your mother prepare yourselves, just to be sure."

Jade nodded. She stood up and shuffled toward the door. "Thanks, Mr. Wakefield," she said.

"I'm sorry, Jade. But remember, he hasn't actually filed anything yet. Maybe he won't. And if he does, your mom has time to get things in order if she starts now."

Jade nodded again, but she couldn't look at him. She was afraid she'd start bawling. Her mother could get it together. Yeah, right. What was she supposed to do, win the lottery?

Jade took a deep breath. "Thanks again," she forced herself to say. "I appreciate the help."

"I'm sorry I didn't have better news. But at least you know what you're up against." He got out of his seat too. "Let me know if he actually does file. I'd be happy to look over his petition and give you more advice if you need it."

"We'd really appreciate that. I'm sure we'll need it," Jade said. She headed out into the hallway, then stopped and turned back toward him. "Would you mind telling Jessica that I had to go home?" she asked. She felt like she'd been socked in the stomach. All she wanted to do was run home and lock herself in her room for the next ten years.

Mr. Wakefield nodded. "Sure, Jade. Good luck."

"Thanks," she whispered, and moved through the living room to let herself out. It sounded like she was going to need some good luck. Luck, and a whopping miracle.

Jessica pulled the embroidered peasant top over her head and frowned at herself in the mirror. From the front the sleeves were definitely too poofy. The dangling price tag caught her eye. She snagged it between her fingers and read it one more time. Was forty-five ninety-nine worth it for a shirt she wasn't deeply in love with?

A quick knock sounded on her door, and before Jessica could respond, the door swung open. Jessica turned, expecting to see Jade, but Elizabeth stood there instead.

"Too poofy," Elizabeth said, wrinkling her nose.

"Yeah, thanks," Jessica said, instantly annoyed. It never helped to hear it from someone else. Especially in the mood she was in.

"Dad wanted me to tell you that Jade had to leave," Elizabeth announced.

"Oh, okay." She was actually relieved. She wasn't in the mood to fake small talk with Jade today.

Elizabeth leaned a shoulder against the door frame and crossed her arms over her chest. "Was that movie you and Jeremy saw any good? I was thinking about asking Maria if she wanted to see a movie later."

"It was okay," Jessica answered.

"Just okay?"

Jessica walked over and plopped down on her bed. "I don't know—I just didn't have a great time last night."

"On a date with your dream man?" Elizabeth's eyes widened. "I thought things were perfect now that you guys are back together."

Jessica sighed. "So did I," she said. "I'm not even sure what happened. It's not like we had a big fight or anything. It's just . . ." She paused, searching for a way to describe it. "We went to dinner at this nice place and then to the movie. It should have been a perfect romantic night, but everything came out wrong. No matter what I said, he said the opposite. We couldn't agree on anything." She traced the blue-and-red pattern around the neck of her blouse. "I told him about what Coach Laufeld did to Annie Whitman, and he practically jumped down my throat about it." She glanced up at her twin, trying to see her reaction. "And then we went to the movie. I hated it, and he loved it. When I tried to say why I didn't like it, he acted like I was an idiot for what I look for in a movie."

Elizabeth rolled her eyes. "Yeah, that does sound horrible. He's got bad taste in movies. You should probably dump him."

"I know it doesn't sound that important, but it feels huge," Jessica protested. This was exactly why she almost hadn't even told her sister anything. There was no way to explain it without sounding petty, but something had just been *off* last night, and she knew Jeremy had felt it too. What if they broke up again?

"I thought we knew each other so well," she tried again, "but now I'm wondering if we really did." Her shoulders sagged, and she looked back at Elizabeth. "Liz, how do you know if somebody's really right for you?"

Elizabeth's expression hardened. She walked farther into the room and sat down at Jessica's desk. "I don't know if it even matters," she said, her tone sharp. "Conner and I were right for each other, and look what happened. Sometimes you're just not good for the person you love, you know? The whole thing just runs out of electricity, like a battery. When it's done, it's done."

Jessica blinked. *Like a battery?* That didn't even sound remotely romantic, which, now that she thought about it, said a whole lot about where her sister's head was at the moment. Jessica flopped backward on the bed. Okay, so getting relationship advice from Ms. Bitter probably wasn't the smartest move at the moment.

"Oh, um, right," Jessica responded. "That's something to think about." *Or not.*

"Yeah," Elizabeth said. "I really think relationships are just up to fate. If it's meant to work, it will, and if it's not . . ."

"The battery thing," Jessica finished for her.

Elizabeth nodded. "Right. So you should try not to worry about it. Whatever happens, happens."

Jessica stretched her arms up over her head. "Thanks for the advice," she said, hoping she didn't sound as sarcastic as she felt.

"Sure," Elizabeth responded. "Well, I better go finish this *Oracle* article," she added before wandering back out of the room.

Jessica stared up at the ceiling. Her stomach felt like it was full of lead. What if all that time she'd spent crying over Jeremy was pointless? What if they just weren't meant for each other?

She covered her eyes with her hands. No, that couldn't be true. There were always sparks between them. The way she remembered it, there were signs right from the beginning that they'd be together. She sifted through scenes in her mind, remembering the way her heart tripped when he smiled at her the first day they worked together at HOJ.

Even their first real date had been an omen. They hadn't meant to end up at the Fantasy Island Fun House, but they'd had an amazing time there. She smiled, thinking about the way he'd insisted on playing that dumb water-pistol game until he'd won her a stuffed animal, even though he could have bought her four by the time he'd done it.

The whole night had been so much fun. It hadn't mattered what kind of movies they liked or how they felt about Coach Laufeld's stupid rules. *Maybe that's what we need,* she realized, sitting up. *To just have fun together again.*

She grabbed the phone off the nightstand and dialed his number.

"Hello?" Jeremy answered after a couple of rings.

"Hi, it's me," Jessica said, trying to sound upbeat.

"Hi, Jess. What's going on?"

Jessica swallowed, her throat suddenly dry. Now that she actually had him on the phone, this wasn't going to sound stupid, was it? No, this was Jeremy. He'd want to go, right? He was as eager as she was to get their relationship back on track. She swallowed again. "Hey, Jeremy, I was wondering—"

"Oh, Jessica, can you hang on a sec?" he asked, interrupting her.

Jessica sighed and closed her eyes in frustration. "Sure."

"Trisha," he yelled in the background. "Get away from the refrigerator. I told you—I'll pour you some orange juice in a second. Okay, sorry," he said into the phone.

"No problem," Jessica lied. "I was just thinking about everything, and, um, I was wondering, do you want to go to the arcade tonight? I've got a serious need to play Skee Ball."

Jeremy laughed. "Skee Ball, huh?"

"Yeah, you know, Skee Ball, bumper cars, Doomslayer." *The things we did together when things were working for us,* she added silently, hoping he'd pick up on her telepathy.

"Can't," he said quickly, as if he hadn't even given her suggestion a thought. "I'm baby-sitting."

"Oh, sure. That's okay. It was just an idea," she said. He didn't sound even slightly sorry that he couldn't go.

I'm probably overreacting, she told herself. So he couldn't go. At least they could have a good conversation. She'd take anything at this point. "Do you have a lot of homework?" she asked.

Jeremy groaned. "I don't even want to think about that; I've got—" He paused. "Hey, Trish, I didn't say you could play outside," he yelled. "Sorry," he said to Jessica. "What were we talking about?"

Jessica felt her jaw tighten. "Nothing important." She closed her eyes, trying to let go of the frustration that was building up inside her. It wasn't his fault the girls were bouncing off the walls today. "So what do you think your team's chances are against North Arlington next week?" she asked.

"I don't know," Jeremy responded. "They've got the biggest defensive line in the league. I'm thinking—"

"Je-re-my," Trisha called out in her high-pitched, little-girl voice. "Emma won't let me turn the channel."

Jeremy sighed into the phone. "Sorry, Jess," he said. "I'd better go."

"Sure," she said. "I'll talk to you later."

She tossed the phone onto her comforter. *That went well,* she thought. *I'd better go. Not I'm dying to talk to you—I'll call you right back.* When they'd first started going out, he would have promised ten times he'd call right back. Now her boyfriend didn't even want to talk to her.

She'd been looking for signs about their relationship. It was starting to seem like they were all pointing in the wrong direction.

Instant Messages

ev-man: Yo, Andy, is that you?

marsden1: No, it's my cyberclone.

ev-man: Ha ha. Let me guess—there's an interactive session of international on-line Tetris going on, right?

marsden1: For your information, I'm logged on to a site for Revolutionary War reenactors. There's a live chat session with some guy who impersonates Thomas Jefferson that starts in five minutes. I'm gonna get all the dirt on Jefferson and turn it into my historical-biography assignment. Piece of cake.

ev-man: Smart man.

marsden1: Yes, I am.

ev-man: So I ran into Jade Wu at the Riot last night.

marsden1: Uh-oh.

ev-man: What does that mean?

marsden1: What did you think of her?

ev-man: She's cute. Very cool.

marsden1: Uh-huh. You're in trouble.

ev-man: What are you talking about?

marsden1: Our little Jade's not a one-guy girl. At least, that's not how

	Jessica tells it. Plus she's
	probably still hung up on
	Jessica's boyfriend, Jeremy.
ev-man:	Another rebound girl? Fabulous.
	Oh, well, I'm not looking for
	that right now anyway.
marsden1:	Uh-huh.
ev-man:	What?
marsden1:	You like her.
ev-man:	Sure, maybe, if I was interested
	in a girlfriend. Which I
	absolutely am not.
marsden1:	You stick with that story.
ev-man:	I'm taking a break from the whole
	relationship area. Completely.
marsden1:	Uh-huh.
ev-man:	Okay, I'm signing off now.
marsden1:	Sure, run back to your Buddhist
	meditation chat.
ev-man:	Actually, I'm checking out
	Britney Spears's Web site, if you
	must know.
marsden1:	Seriously?
ev-man:	What do you think?
marsden1:	Right. Hey, looks like this
	Jefferson guy is getting ready to
	talk—I better get back to the
	chat room.
ev-man:	Ciao.

CHAPTER

new Initials

5

Squeak, squeak, squeak. Will cringed at the sound the rubber tips of his crutches made on the area of the floor where the carpet had peeled away. *This sucks,* he thought as he inched his way down the crowded hall toward his second-period class on Monday morning. Bodies zoomed around him right and left, dodging him as if he were a car stalled in the middle of the freeway. He concentrated on trying to get into a rhythm with his stupid crutches, but the weight of his backpack swinging from his shoulder as he moved kept throwing him off.

Someone clipped him hard from behind, shoving him sideways. He threw out his left arm to catch his balance, and his crutch went flying. Before he could steady himself, his backpack slid off and skidded into a locker with a loud bang.

"Damn," he yelled. He tilted sideways and almost fell over, but between his one crutch and his good leg, he managed to get his balance back.

The crowd parted around him, making a bubble of space between him and his things. People slowed down, as if staring at a car wreck, their mouths turned down in sympathetic grimaces. What was he supposed to do now? His crutch lay about five feet away underneath his backpack, and with his cast he couldn't bend down to pick anything up.

Will's chest tightened with anger. He glared at a group of freshman boys who were looking at him with pity in their eyes. He didn't need sympathy. Not from any of these geeks.

"Don't worry. I've got this."

Will looked up. A petite blond girl with a round face was smiling at him, offering his crutch. Will smiled back and took it. "Thanks," he said.

"No problem." She turned, picked up his backpack, and held it out to him. Will shifted his weight, afraid that if he swung his backpack back on, he'd topple over.

The girl took a step back. "Stick out your arm," she told him. "I'll slip this on." She was so close, Will could smell her light perfume. Somehow this time he didn't mind the help. He held out his left arm and waited for her to hitch his backpack up onto his shoulder. "There." She patted his shoulder and stepped back.

Will nodded in thanks. He couldn't help noticing that she had that impressed look in her eyes, the awed, starry-eyed look he was used to getting when he came off the football field. The look he missed. Will grinned at her.

She immediately blushed. "So you're okay?" she asked.

Will nodded. "Yeah, I'm okay, thanks."

"Sure." She twisted her fingers around a strand of honey-colored hair. "So could I, you know, sign your cast?" she asked shyly.

Will's grin broadened. "You bet."

"Wow, cool," she said. She dug into her backpack for a marker.

Will watched the people heading down the hall, staring at him while she knelt in front of him and wrote a message on the cast. He tilted up his chin. Now he didn't mind the focus on him. He wasn't some pathetic guy hobbling around—he was the wounded jock getting attention from a pretty girl. This was the way his life at SVH was supposed to be. Well, with one major difference.

She stood up and capped the marker. "I better get to class," she said. "Maybe I'll see you around."

"Yeah, see you," Will replied. He looked down at the signature once she'd left.

Will,
  You're a great quarterback. SVH needs you. Get well soon!!!
                                      Cindi

He gripped the handles of his crutches hard so he wouldn't lose his balance and turned his foot slowly from side to side, admiring the words. The rest of the cast was still white—blank—but he could visualize it covered in multicolored ink, with messages from a bunch of other girls, all saying how great he was and how he should be back playing football. Maybe this cast wouldn't be so bad for a while. It had its benefits, at least.

He started his slow progress down the hall again. The crutches were still awkward, and he had to keep most of his attention focused on the floor in front of him so he wouldn't put a crutch down on a piece of paper and slip. But even without looking he sensed he was closing in on Melissa's locker. He glanced up as he got closer, unable to help himself.

His gaze landed on a couple in a full-on lip lock. The guy had the girl backed up against the lockers. All Will could see were her arms around his neck beneath his close-cropped blond hair.

Will took in a sharp breath as he realized what he was seeing. Melissa's arms. *Melissa's.* Around Ken Matthews's neck.

Will stopped moving. His entire body felt hot and shaky all at the same time. He blinked, thinking he might actually hurl right there in the hallway.

At that moment Melissa pulled away from Ken

and looked to the side—right into Will's furious gaze. Her mouth dropped open for a second, and her eyes filled with that familiar soft, tender vulnerability that used to make him weak. Then she recovered, and her typical cool, in-control expression replaced whatever attempt at emotion she'd had there.

Ken must have noticed the shift in her attitude, though, because he backed up a few steps and turned to see where she was looking. The instant he saw Will, his face paled, and he moved farther away from Melissa, stuffing his hands in the pockets of his jeans.

Will stood perfectly still while his heart pounded in his chest. He struggled to get his brain to work and give him a way out of this situation without losing all pride.

As if there was anything he could do. He couldn't smash Ken's face into a locker. He couldn't even stalk away. Not on the crutches. But there was one option, one way to make sure they couldn't see all the anger and humiliation he could feel plastered across his face. Slowly he turned his back on them, making it clear he was in no rush. His head down, his gaze focused on the littered hallway, he stumped his way carefully back down the hallway, the way he had come. Forget second period. He wasn't in the mood to deal with class now.

He'd just turned the corner when he heard a girl's voice behind him, calling his name. "Will, wait up."

He flinched, barely able to even wonder if it was Melissa before realizing that wasn't her voice. He planted his crutches wide so he could look back over his shoulder.

When he saw the shoulder-length blond hair, his eyes widened in surprise. *Jessica Wakefield?*

She skidded to a stop next to him, the heels of her platform shoes clacking as she moved. "Hey," she said. "Are you all right?"

"Oh, yeah, I'm great," Will answered, unable to hold back the bitterness. He clutched the crutch handles in a death grip, waiting for Jessica to slam him too. She must have loved watching him humiliated like that, even if it was by Melissa.

Jessica winced. "I saw what happened back there, and I just wanted you to know that it was really wrong. You didn't deserve that." She stopped and took a deep breath, avoiding meeting his gaze directly. "I know I can't really help. I just . . . it just stinks."

Will swallowed hard, trying to clear the emotions swirling in his head. "Thanks," he finally said.

Jessica gave him a tiny smile, then glanced around her awkwardly. "So, yeah, I just wanted you to know that," she said. She turned and took off, disappearing into the crowd.

Will leaned back against a row of lockers. Jessica, on his side? After the way things had gone between the two of them, that was not something he would have bet on. Although maybe she did hate Melissa even more than she hated him. Or maybe he was just *that* pathetic now.

"Okay, class, let's look at what we get if we graph the relationship of A to the third power plus B to the third power." Ms. Dixon turned her back to sketch out a graph on the board.

Melissa watched her draw lines on the board but didn't even lift her pencil to copy them down. She knew she should be thinking about Ken, about the way he'd backed her up against her locker and kissed her right in front of everybody.

But she wasn't. She was thinking about Will. About the horrified expression on his face. The obvious, raw pain in his eyes.

Not good. Not good at all.

Melissa glared at the dark square of ink on the cover of her notebook that covered up the heart with *W + M 4-ever* in the middle. She grabbed her pencil and started filling in the ink even darker. She didn't need to care about what Will thought anymore. They were done; she'd moved on. End of story.

So he'd seen them kissing. So what? It was bound

to happen sooner or later, right? She'd run into the same thing eventually.

Melissa sucked in a surprised breath. *Wow.* The thought of Will kissing someone else made her stomach clench.

While Ms. Dixon hovered over her open math book, checking on the next problem, Cherie slid a note onto her desk. Melissa sighed, then glanced down at what her friend had written.

> *Hey,*
> *We're on #12 . . . wake up, girl. I need your brain!!!*

Melissa crumpled up the note and gave Cherie a quick nod. Yeah, she'd better pay attention. No way was she going to explain to Cherie that she was having any thoughts at all about Will Simmons. She had no excuse to be distracted.

She quickly finished filling in the rest of the problem Ms. Dixon had just laid out on the board and tilted her paper toward Cherie so she could copy the answer.

"And now on number thirteen, let's see who can show me what happens when we add C to the third power to the equation," Ms. Dixon droned.

Melissa turned her paper back toward herself and filled in a new graph for the problem. Okay, so she wouldn't think about Will anymore. She wouldn't think about how hurt he'd looked in the hall or about how right they'd been for each other.

She'd think about Ken, about what a good kisser he was . . . but so was Will. Melissa closed her eyes. It took no effort at all to imagine Will's strong arms around her or the way his lips moved over hers. Or the way he always smelled like soap . . . or the way his hair felt damp beneath her fingers when they'd kiss after he drove her home from practice every day.

No. Melissa sat up straight. She was supposed to be daydreaming about Ken, about the way *he* kissed, about the way his shorter, coarser hair felt beneath her fingertips.

Ken, her boyfriend—not Will, her ex, the guy on his way to nowhere.

Across from her Cherie tilted her own notebook in Melissa's direction and tapped it with her pencil, frowning.

Melissa glanced at the writing in the margin.

Hey—
   Where are you today? We're on #14!!!

"Sorry," she mouthed silently to Cherie, and squinted at the board, trying to pick up the problem where she'd drifted off. She swept her brown hair back off her face and bent her head over her paper, trying to let the numbers make sense. But in her mind she kept picturing Will's face when he'd seen them kissing. And worse than that, she imagined the glare Jessica Wakefield had given her before taking off after Will. Melissa stiffened. Jessica and Will? She'd never thought about that. Now that he was free again, was it possible Jessica would get tired of her boring Big Mesa boyfriend and come running back to Will? Melissa gripped her pencil so tightly, her fingers started to ache.

"Melissa!" Cherie's whisper jarred her back to reality. "What's up with you?"

Melissa quickly gathered herself together. No way was she going to let Cherie or anybody else know where her mind had been. She gave her friend a bored look and kicked her brain into gear. "I was just thinking about that black skirt I got last week," she said, her eye on Ms. Dixon, who was still writing on the board. "Should I wear it with my black platforms or flats?"

Cherie eyed the teacher too. "Platforms," she answered.

Melissa nodded. "That's what I was thinking."

"Okay, who thinks they have number fifteen correct?" Ms. Dixon asked the class, swiveling around to face them.

Melissa slunk down in her seat, careful not to make eye contact. She hadn't even copied down the problem yet. *Okay,* she told herself. *It's okay to have some feelings for Will.* Of course she did. They'd been a couple forever. Erasing him from her mind was going to take time. But she'd get it done because she had to. Will was nothing now, and she couldn't let herself be nothing with him.

She dragged her notebook toward her and pulled a blue pen out of her backpack. She hesitated for a moment, and then she sketched a big, bold heart. In the middle she filled in new initials.

MF and KM 4-ever.

Please don't let this be about Mom, Jade begged silently as she rushed down the hall toward the school social worker's office.

She'd been ready to fall asleep in fourth-period study hall when she'd been called down to the office to see the social worker, Mrs. Delbanco. And she could think of only one reason: Her mother had been taken to the hospital again. Panic made her hands shake as she rounded the corner and hurried toward Mrs. Delbanco's open door.

Mrs. Delbanco smiled as soon as she caught sight of Jade in the doorway. "Jade, come in."

Too nervous to answer, Jade just nodded and slipped through the door. She sat on the very edge of the orange plastic chair facing the social worker's desk and set her full backpack on her knees, as if it could somehow shield her from the bad news she figured she was about to get.

Mrs. Delbanco sat back in her swivel chair and

took off her wire-framed reading glasses. She was a large, round, motherly looking woman who dressed in flowing, caftanlike dresses that Jade guessed were supposed to make people feel at ease somehow.

It certainly wasn't working for her.

"I got an unusual phone call a few minutes ago, Jade," Mrs. Delbanco began. "From your father."

"My father?" Jade echoed. "Why would—" She cut herself off. Oh, her father. It took a second for her to realize this had nothing to do with her mom's health and everything to do with her entire future.

Images of her mother lying on a gurney in the emergency room disappeared, replaced by a picture of her stupid, uptight father looking down his nose at her. *God, he barely waited at all,* she thought, a new panic settling over her. *He's really going to do this!*

She hugged her backpack to her chest and inched backward in her seat, buying a few seconds until she could figure out something intelligent to say.

"Your father seems very concerned about your welfare," Mrs. Delbanco explained. Her eyes flicked over Jade, as if she was checking to see that Jade was in one piece.

"I'm fine," Jade assured her. "There's no reason for him to worry about me."

"That's not what he thinks." Her lips pursed as she gave Jade a long look. "He seems worried that you don't have any supervision at home."

"How would he know?" Jade snapped. "He lives in another state."

"You sound angry," Mrs. Delbanco observed.

Jade clutched her backpack. "Yeah, I'm mad. He's not even part of my life. He hates my mother, and so he thinks he can just show up and start tearing her down." She flopped back in her chair. "He's a jerk."

Mrs. Delbanco nodded, clasping her hands in front of her. "Jade, I understand your mother's been sick lately. Is she—"

"My mom's fine now," Jade cut her off. "She got sick because she's had to work so hard since my father barely helps us. But she's fine now," she repeated.

"I see." Mrs. Delbanco's lips curved in a small, insincere smile. "Is she still working a second job?"

"She has to."

Mrs. Delbanco consulted the open file in front of her. "Her full-time job is at a bank, isn't that right?"

Jade nodded.

"What kinds of hours does she work at her other job?"

Jade opened her mouth to answer, then stopped. What was she supposed to say? What would make her mother sound responsible? "She works just a couple of afternoons a week," she said finally.

Mrs. Delbanco's eyebrows raised. "Your father

seems to think she's gone a lot in the evenings."

"My father was here only a couple of days," Jade explained. "He doesn't know."

"He feels he knows enough to be concerned about you."

"That's his problem." Jade could feel the anger growing inside her. She wanted to call him up right this minute and scream at him to leave her alone.

"So your mother is home in the evenings."

"Sure," Jade answered, shifting uneasily.

"So if she works full-time at the bank, then when does she work this other job again?"

"At night," Jade answered without thinking. Then she realized what she'd just said. She glared at the social worker. "Okay, so she works a couple of nights a week," she confessed. "It's no big deal. I'm not even home most of the time anyway."

Mrs. Delbanco's thick eyebrows shot up. "Oh?"

"I mean, I go to work too. We need the money." She winced. "I mean, I like to have money to spend on extra stuff."

Mrs. Delbanco wasn't even focusing on Jade anymore. She was staring at Jade's file. Jade wiped her sweating palms on the legs of her brown corduroy pants. She needed to calm down if she wanted to avoid getting tripped up again.

Finally the social worker sat straight up and flashed

Jade a smile that was probably supposed to appear sincere and helpful. Jade crossed her arms over her chest. Right, like she was going to believe that.

"This is too important to let go," Mrs. Delbanco said. "And I don't want things to get out of hand. I believe the best thing to do under the circumstances is for all of us to get together and see if we can sort out what's going on."

Jade let out a frustrated sigh.

Mrs. Delbanco frowned. "I understand your frustration, Jade, but I think your father may have a point. And if we can all sit down and talk this out like adults, we may be able to keep this whole issue out of the court system. Now, that sounds like the best way to go, doesn't it?"

No, Jade thought. *The best way to go is to tell my father to leave us alone.* But that wasn't going to happen. He'd already called the school. He was really serious about all of this. And of course she'd rather resolve things here than in court, but getting her mother and father in the same room would only make it worse.

You can have your meeting, she thought, glaring at Mrs. Delbanco, *but it's going to blow up in your face. And more important—in mine.*

Jessica Wakefield

It's amazing how much I don't care about Will Simmons anymore. Really. All I feel for the guy is pity. It's horrible to see anybody in that much pain. Even him. Yeah, he turned on me when he had the chance, and he's a selfish — make that megaselfish — jock. But nobody deserves to go through this.

I mean, he's lost everything he cares about — football, status, even Melissa. Then he has to watch her making out in the hall with the guy who won it all?

That is beyond torture.

A month ago I would have been the first one laughing if I'd seen the look on his face when he caught Melissa and Ken's little scene. Now it just makes me sad.

CHAPTER 6
Like Watching a Car Accident

Jessica scrubbed vigorously at the dried milk caking the steam wand of HOJ's espresso maker. Normally she hated cleaning, but today it felt good to keep her hands active, busy. That way she couldn't worry as much about every word she exchanged with Jeremy. Luckily the manual-labor-distraction thing was turning out not to be too necessary—they'd been getting along really well this whole shift.

She glanced over in Jeremy's direction. He was filling stainless-steel pitchers with cold milk and putting them in the minirefrigerator under the counter. "Wasn't Corey supposed to do that?" he asked her, pointing at the steam wand.

Jessica shrugged. "Yeah, whatever. It's no big deal."

Jeremy raised his eyebrows. "You're feeling generous today, Ms. Assistant Manager."

Jessica giggled. "I guess I am."

Jeremy leaned in closer to her. "Did you see Corey's friends?" he asked, nodding at a group of guys and girls hanging around the coffee shop's front door. Jessica had noticed them, but she focused in more closely now. They all looked the same—nose rings, eyebrow rings, spiked hair in a rainbow of colors, and dark, baggy clothing.

"They look like refugees from some alien planet," she commented in a low voice.

Jeremy laughed. "No kidding. Are any of her friends normal?" he whispered. His breath on her ear made a little shiver slide down the back of her neck.

Jessica giggled in return. "Those *are* her normal friends," she shot back.

Jeremy rolled his eyes, and Jessica smiled up at him. This felt good. Great, actually. Like they were back in sync. Like maybe all the tension between them the past couple of days really didn't matter.

The bells on the front door jingled, catching Jessica's attention. Corey's friends stepped aside, making room for someone to enter. Jessica squinted and saw . . . Melissa Fox. Great. Just what she needed when things had been going so well with Jeremy. Jessica winced, then froze when she saw Ken holding the door for Melissa. They had come here together? How could Ken bring that girl here?

Melissa moved into the room the way she always did—with attitude and arrogance, surveying the area to see if there was anyone worthy of her attention.

Ken followed her, his hand resting protectively against the small of her back.

Gross. Jessica threw down the sponge, then glanced at Jeremy to catch his reaction, but he had his head in the pastry case already, rearranging the cookies.

When Ken and Melissa reached the counter, Ken smiled at Jessica over the jars of biscotti as if nothing was wrong. "Hey," he said.

She paused, narrowing her eyes slightly. "Hi," she responded. She made sure to keep her expression neutral as she stepped over to the cash register. She wanted Ken to know she was angry, but she definitely didn't want Melissa to think she'd gotten to her. Ken stared up at the menu behind her as if he'd never seen it before. So obviously he wasn't as comfortable as he was trying to act. He felt weird about being here with Melissa, in front of Jessica.

Well, he should, she thought. He should be totally ashamed to show up here with her biggest enemy after he'd dumped one of Jessica's friends.

Jessica's gaze switched to Melissa, just for a second, but she caught Melissa's eyes flickering over her. Melissa's lips curved into her trademark smirk, giving Jessica the intended message—she'd won.

Jessica folded her arms across her chest and looked Melissa right in the eye. "Do you know what you want?"

"Sure," Ken said quickly, still staring up at the board. "Um, yeah. I'll have a tall mocha."

Melissa leaned into Ken and wrapped her hands around his arm. She pressed her cheek against his arm, still staring at Jessica. "I want carrot cake," she said, "and a double cappuccino."

And I want to puke, Jessica thought. She grabbed a pad of paper and scribbled down their order. Then she rang it up. "That's eight fifty-six," she said flatly.

Ken scrambled to pull out his wallet, which wasn't so easy with Melissa stuck to his arm like a barnacle. Melissa didn't make a move. Of course. In the world according to Melissa, guys were made to serve. *Everyone* was made to serve, actually.

Jessica pulled Ken's change out of the cash drawer and handed it to him as quickly as she could, hoping Ken would get the hint and drink his coffee faster than he ever had before.

"Thanks," Ken said. He turned and held out his hand for Melissa. She wrapped her fingers around his, and they wove their way between the tables— holding hands the whole time.

Ken, holding hands with Melissa Fox. This was too twisted. An image of Will's stricken face in school this morning flashed through Jessica's mind. And worse, the mournful look that had been plastered on Maria's face constantly ever since she'd broken up with Ken. At least Maria wasn't here to watch this gag fest of affection.

A tap on her shoulder made her jump.

"Sorry, I didn't mean to scare you." Jeremy grinned at her. "I'm going to go in the back and see if we have any more blueberry muffins."

Muffins. Right. That was important when a supposed friend of hers had just dumped another friend of hers to go out with the school witch. Were guys completely oblivious to everything that went on, or was it just Jeremy?

"Uh, yeah, okay," she replied without taking her gaze away from the happy couple. They settled into a small table near the back, and as soon as Melissa had slid into the chair next to Ken's, she inched closer to snuggle against him. Ken wrapped an arm over Melissa's shoulders and pulled her tight. It was like watching a car accident. She knew the sight would make her sick, but she couldn't tear her eyes away.

Still, she couldn't just stand here either. She grabbed a pitcher of milk and shoved it under the steam wand on the espresso maker, sneaking peeks at Ken and Melissa every few seconds. She moved the pitcher up and down, letting the steam rush through the cold milk with a loud, angry whoosh.

How had Ken managed to lose all control of his mind?

Melissa laid her hand on Ken's thigh. "So how was practice today?" she asked.

"Fine," he answered. Actually, it hadn't been. He was still messing up those easy passes. Something was just off with his arm, and he didn't know what it was. He cast a quick glance over at Jessica, who was slamming things around behind the counter. She was definitely not happy to see him here with Melissa. It wasn't a huge surprise, but it was still annoying. He and Jessica had been friends for a long time. Yeah, she and Melissa didn't get along—but that didn't mean she had to suddenly treat him like a stranger.

Ken stared down at the brown lumps of raw sugar in the glass bowl on their table. He tightened his arm around Melissa's shoulders, wishing their drinks would come soon. Coming here had been a mistake. He'd wanted to test things out, see where things stood with his friends. He hadn't really hung out with anyone except Melissa and his teammates since he'd broken up with Maria. But now he knew the deal. He wasn't part of their silly little group anymore, and that was it.

Melissa pulled away from him. "I'm going to run

to the bathroom before our drinks get here," she said. She smiled, then got up and began heading over to the rest rooms.

Ken stared out across the room, his eyes glazing over. He wondered if he should go up to the counter and talk to Jessica alone. He shoved the sugar bowl away from him. This was so lame. He and Jessica knew each other way before he dated Maria. Now he had to worry about everything—who he talked to, what he said. Would Jessica just get more angry if he said something? Would Melissa freak if she came out of the bathroom and saw him with Jessica?

Things had gotten way too complicated, way too quickly.

Suddenly two cups were slammed down on the table in front of him, jerking him out of his thoughts. "Here are your drinks," Jessica announced, her voice icy.

Ken looked up, startled. "Hey, Jessica, thanks." He cleared his throat, trying to think of what to say before she walked off, but he couldn't come up with anything.

Jessica didn't reply, but she didn't go anywhere either. She just stood there, her hands on her hips, her mouth set in a tight line. Her cheeks had a slight pink tinge to them too, he noticed. She was seriously ticked off.

"So, uh, how's it going?" he finally asked.

She let out a short laugh. "How's it going? Oh, that's something." She paused. "Look, I know it's not my business," she blurted out, "but how could you even think of dumping Maria for somebody like— like *her*. Don't you have any clue what she's like?"

"Jessica, you don't know her—"

"Oh, right, I don't." Jessica slid into the seat across from him and leaned forward over the table. "You know what she did to me," she said in a low, harsh voice. "She only got half the school to believe I'm the slut of the century. But I don't know her." She pushed the sugar bowl in Ken's direction. "Right."

Ken bit his lower lip. If he could just get Jessica and his other friends to see that Melissa could be a totally different person than they'd seen . . .

"Okay," he said, "so you know one side of her, but she's got a lot more to her. She can be—"

"What, even more of a witch than she's been to me?" Jessica cut him off. "After today I'll believe that."

Ken grabbed the sugar bowl and wrapped his fingers around it. "What are you talking about?"

"Just that little incident with Will in the hall. Have you forgotten your little make-out session already?" Jessica picked up a spoon and started

106

tapping it on the table. "I never, *ever* thought I'd feel sorry for Will Simmons, but what you and Melissa did today was beyond low. Couldn't you have been *slightly* more sympathetic on the guy's first day back at school?"

Ken sank back in his seat and crossed his arms over his chest. Now he really had no clue what to say.

Jessica dropped the spoon. It clattered across the table and hit Ken's fingers. She got up from her seat. "You know, now that I think about it, maybe you're not the person I thought you were either. Maybe you and Melissa deserve each other." Before Ken could open his mouth, she had turned and stalked back toward the counter.

Ken watched her hair bounce as she huffed off. Her angry words rang in his ears like a cannon blast after a football game. He stared at the drinks on the table, then at Melissa's empty seat. He knew Jessica was overreacting, so why did her speech still leave him feeling like a jerk?

Jade hurried between the tables at Guido's, leading a family of four to their booth. The long, black rayon skirt she had to wear for hostessing clung to her legs every time she took a step, driving her crazy. Of course, everything today was driving her crazy. Ever since that meeting with stupid Mrs. Delbanco.

She seated the family, distributed the big, plastic-laminated menus, and turned on her heel, hoping she could get a chance to sit down at the hostess's station for a minute before the next crowd of diners came in.

She needed the break. Ever since study hall, all she could think about was having to face her father. There was nothing she could do about it, but that didn't help. She'd been jumpy all day and constantly on the verge of a panic attack. And now she had to get through a long shift at her new job.

"Miss?" A woman in a tight-fitting business suit waved at Jade to flag her down.

"Yes?" Jade smiled automatically, stepping over to the table. "What can I get for you?"

The woman glared at her. "We specifically asked to be seated in nonsmoking," she snapped.

Jade's shoulders slumped. "Oh, I'm so sorry." She whirled around, automatically checking the tables on the other side of the restaurant. *Great.* There were no open tables in the nonsmoking section. She cleared her throat. "It looks like it'll be, um, a few minutes," she said tentatively. "If you wouldn't mind—"

The woman looked at the other two ladies at the table and rolled her eyes. "I guess we don't have a choice, then. We'll stay here until you get us a new table."

108

Jade tried to smile at her. "Thank you. I'll get you the next table that's free." She hurried back to the hostess's station and climbed up onto the stool next to the cash register. God, what else was she going to mess up tonight?

"We need a table."

Jade looked up to see a tall, gaunt man with graying hair standing in front of her. Behind him was a petite woman wearing a mousy brown dress. "For two?" she asked automatically.

The man sneered at her. "No kidding."

"O-kaay," Jade drawled, instantly irritated by the man's rudeness.

She took her time getting off the stool and picking up a couple of menus. This was not what she needed tonight on top of everything else—an obnoxious jerk. "If you'll follow me," she said, then led them to a table for two across from the kitchen.

"This is a terrible table," the man barked. "I want that one over there." He pointed toward a six-person booth in the back corner.

Jade gripped the menus so tightly, she felt them bend between her fingers. It was a good thing she wouldn't be his waitress. He'd be wearing his dinner.

"I'm sorry, sir, but that isn't possible," she said. She handed the woman her menu first, and as she went to give the man his, he snatched it out of her fingers. Jade ground her teeth together, trying hard not to let him get to her. "We've got several specials tonight," she said, launching into her normal script.

"Yeah? Any of them good?" the man shot back.

All of Jade's anger and frustration spilled over. "No," she said before she could stop herself, "they're all terrible."

The man's head jerked back, and he stared at her, his mouth hanging open. Jade wanted to laugh. Instead she turned and stalked back to the hostess's station. She was just getting ready to sit back down when Mr. Martin, the manager, walked up. He stabbed a finger toward the kitchen doors. "I want to talk to you. Now," he commanded, and headed off.

Jade's heart started pounding. Oh God, he hadn't heard her talking to that man, had he? She followed him, her knees shaking with each step.

Once she got through the swinging doors, he was waiting for her, next to a prep table piled with boxes of lettuce. "That was completely out of line," he said, his voice sharp with anger. "There is no excuse for talking to a customer like that. None."

Jade's face reddened. She sagged back against the stainless-steel table. "I know. I—"

"I don't want to hear it," he interrupted her. His gray eyes were barely visible, his face was drawn so tight with anger. "If I ever, *ever* hear you talking to a patron like that again, you will be out of here so fast. . . ."

Jade's lower lip trembled. "I won't," she choked out. "I—" She started to explain, but her throat closed up. What was she going to say anyway? *My father is going to destroy my life?* Mr. Martin wasn't going to care about that.

She tried taking a couple of slow, deep breaths, but every time she inhaled, the pressure in her chest just got tighter and tighter. "I won't cause any more problems," she said.

"You better not," he said. "This is absolutely your last warning."

Jade nodded and tried to swallow the sharp lump in her throat. "I understand."

Panic made her feel light-headed. She could not lose this job. She couldn't, not after getting fired twice now. She was going to cry; she could feel it. "Excuse me," she whispered, then took off for the bathroom.

The instant she pushed open the door, the harsh, flowery scent of disinfectant clogged her nose. Her stomach tightened, and for a minute she thought she was going to be sick. But the wave of nausea passed. She bolted for the corner stall and locked herself inside. Then she sank down on the toilet seat and buried her face in her hands.

Tears slid down her cheeks, and she didn't even attempt to stop them. Her father hadn't even sued for custody yet, and he was already messing things up for her. He was really going to do this. He was going to take her away from her mother, the only stable person she'd ever had in her life. Oh, and on top of that she was going to lose her third job in a row.

Jade stared at the graffiti scratched into the stall door. The comments moved in and out of focus as tears swam in front of her eyes. What had she done to deserve a parent like him?

The bathroom door opened, and someone entered the stall next to her. Jade grabbed a handful of toilet paper and quietly blew her nose. She had to get herself back together. Mr. Martin was probably pacing back and forth by the front door, timing her bathroom break. Besides, she couldn't hang out in the rest room the whole night.

The woman in the stall next to her flushed the toilet and left. Jade came out of her stall. She wiped the tears from her cheeks and blew her nose one more time. Then she crossed to the sink and splashed cold water on her face until she decided it didn't look quite as red and blotchy. Finally she ran her fingers through her hair to straighten it and stepped back outside.

She almost made it back to the hostess's station,

but one glance at the rude jerk in the corner booth made all the feelings slam back down on top of her.

Instead of heading up front, she veered left, toward the manager's office. She couldn't do this. Not tonight. Not for three more hours. She had to go home. If they fired her, they fired her.

Mr. Martin was sitting at his desk, straightening a pile of cash-register receipts. He looked up, frowning, when he heard Jade approach.

She wrapped her arms across her stomach. "Mr. Martin?" she said. "I have to go home. I'm—I don't feel well."

The manager stroked the edges of his dark mustache with his finger. He heaved a huge sigh. "I can't tell you to stay," he said. "But this better be a onetime thing. I won't have people here I can't depend on."

Jade shook her head. "It won't happen again. It— It won't," she assured him.

He waved her out. "Don't miss your next shift," he said, and turned back to his work.

No, Jade thought, she wouldn't. She couldn't. Somehow she would go home and figure out how to function under all this stress.

And she'd try to figure out how to keep her father from taking away everything that mattered.

Elizabeth Wakefield

Ever since Jessica was bugging me the other day about her and Jeremy, I've been wondering about what I told her. It's funny—just because I used to be long-term-relationship girl, people seem to think I'm some kind of expert on this stuff. I guess I know the basics. True love is about caring for someone more than you care about yourself. It's about finding your soul mate, the person who completes you and makes you more than you are on your own.

You're supposed to know it when you feel it, but I'm not sure. I _thought_ I felt it with Todd, and I was wrong there. I even thought I felt it with Jeffrey French! Then there was Conner, and that was a totally different level. It

seemed more real than anything before.
But now even that turned out not to
be true. But hey, at least I can say I
know what true love _doesn't_ feel like.
That's something, right?

CHAPTER
Show No Weakness
7

Jeremy tuned in to the slow reggae tune playing on the radio as he poured a five-pound bag of French-roast beans into the top of the coffee grinder. The light music didn't fit his mood at all. He couldn't stop wondering what had happened between Jessica and Ken a few minutes ago to get her so upset. He'd come out from the back in time to see them talking and then watched as Jessica stormed away from the table.

He knew it shouldn't be a big deal, but things had been so touchy with Jessica lately, it was easy to feel paranoid. He knew how Jessica felt about Melissa Fox, Ken's date, and he knew that it all went back to one person—Will Simmons. Not someone he wanted to believe Jessica still cared about.

Jeremy flipped on the grinder and watched while the machine sucked down the beans and spit them out into the plastic container in the bottom. He really wanted to ask Jessica what went down with Ken. But what if he asked and it turned into another fight? It seemed like things were just starting to feel okay again between them. Maybe it wasn't worth the risk.

Suddenly two hands grabbed his sides and squeezed. He whirled around and saw Jessica grinning up at him. "Thanks. Give me a heart attack, why don't you," he teased.

Jessica laughed. "Got you."

"Yeah, okay." Jeremy laughed too. He couldn't help it. "I owe you one, though."

"I'm counting on it," she replied, raising her eyebrows slightly.

Jeremy gulped. When Jessica wanted to turn on the charm, he felt completely helpless . . . in a completely great sort of way.

The beans weren't finished grinding yet, but he switched off the machine anyway. If he didn't ask her now, it was just going to bother him until he did. "So what was that all about with Ken before?" he asked.

Jessica's smile tightened, and she moved her gaze away from his. "Nothing," she said.

Jeremy frowned. "Nothing? Then why were you taking all your aggressions out on the coffee filters?" he asked, pointing at the stack of filters that she'd been tossing around a second ago.

Jessica pushed a few strands of hair back behind her ears. "Okay, I guess we were kind of fighting," she admitted. "I sort of—I said something to him about the way he and Melissa are acting. You should have seen the look on Will's face today when he saw . . ." She stopped, obviously noticing the look on *Jeremy's* face.

How could she get like this over Will? He'd actually believed she was over the guy, but maybe she never would be. "So let me get this straight," he said through clenched teeth. "You reamed out your *friend* Ken because of Will Simmons?"

Jessica scrunched up her face. "I know that sounds bad," she said, "but it's not what you're thinking."

"Yeah, it sounds bad," Jeremy said. He leaned back against the sink counter and folded his arms across his chest. "And I don't know how it couldn't be what I'm thinking. You're worried about some guy who let the whole school think you were a slut, then broke your heart." *And took you away from me.*

Jessica groaned. "No, that's not it. Will Simmons is a complete jerk. I agree. But this isn't about him. Not really."

"Sure sounds like it is," he said, turning his back on her.

"Would you listen to me?" Jessica pleaded over his shoulder. "I expect Melissa to treat people like garbage, but I never expected Ken to be such a jerk.

You saw them in here. And this morning in the hallway it was like he was rubbing it in Will's face how he has everything now that Will lost."

Jeremy spun back around. "But this isn't about Will, huh?" he said sarcastically. He shook his head.

Jessica rolled her eyes. "I can't stand Will, okay? I swear. But it's just not right for anybody to be treated like that. Not even him."

Jeremy gripped the counter behind him. He wanted to believe her, but it didn't sound good. Not at all. Besides, why did Will need her to be his protector? The guy could look out for himself.

Jessica reached out and took his hands in hers. "Look," she said, staring straight into his eyes. "I'm not explaining this very well." She squeezed his hands. "I'm just mad that a guy I thought was a friend could be so cold. I mean, it's not just Will getting hurt. Maria's a mess too, and I *do* care about her. And I always thought Ken was a good guy. I can't deal with watching him ruin everything like this."

Jeremy took a deep breath. "I can see where Ken's being a jerk," he began, "but I still don't get why you need to be involved here."

Jessica frowned. "Because Maria and Ken are my friends," she explained.

Jeremy shrugged. "Yeah, but relationships always

get messy. I don't go off on Trent or Stan when they have problems with their girlfriends. Why can't you just let it go?"

"I'm sorry, but if I think my friends need me, then I'm not going to just *let it go.*" Jessica brushed past him and grabbed the open bag of coffee beans. With sharp, quick motions she rolled down the top and shoved the bag back onto the lower shelf.

Jeremy followed her. "How do you even know they need you?" he shot back. "Are they asking for your help? Is Will? What if you don't know the whole story?"

Jessica's head snapped back. "What are you saying?"

"I just don't think that getting in the middle of other people's relationships is a good idea."

Jessica straightened. "So you wouldn't be willing to step in and help your friends if they were in trouble?"

"I didn't say that," Jeremy said. "And I don't think it makes me a bad friend anyway just because I want to let my friends work things out for themselves."

Jessica's eyes blazed. "I'm not *interfering,* if that's what you're getting at. I just need to tell someone if they're acting like a jerk."

"Yeah, well, you sure feel like you need to do that an awful lot," he snapped.

Jessica blinked, and Jeremy felt a twinge of guilt. "Maybe I'm just a better friend than you are," she said, quickly recovering.

He shook his head. "Thanks, Jess. Thanks a lot." He looked up at the clock over the espresso maker. "I'm taking a break," he said. He turned and headed for the employee lounge in the back.

All of his muscles felt stiff as he sank down onto the sofa. So he and Jessica had managed to get along for a whole half of a shift. Great. What did *that* say about their relationship?

Will limped through the front door of his house and dropped his backpack onto the floor. Gingerly he pulled the crutches out from under his sore armpits and set them next to him. He leaned back against the door and groaned, his eyes closed. His hands were shaking with fatigue, and his leg was throbbing. With every step he felt like he was being stabbed in the knee with a hot knife. A whole day at school had definitely been more than he could handle.

And that didn't even count that little scene with Melissa.

"Hi, Will," his mother called out from the kitchen. "Your father and I are having a drink in the backyard. Why don't you join us?"

Will groaned again and tried to flex his bad leg to ease the tightness in his hip. *No, thanks. I think I'll just die right here.*

Footsteps moved across the kitchen toward him. "Will?" his mother asked.

Will snapped open his eyes. His mother was coming through the living room, drying her hands on a kitchen towel. Her expression was tight with worry. "How did school go?" she asked.

Will pushed himself away from the door. *Show no weakness,* he thought automatically. If he was going to get back on the football field, he couldn't let anyone see him struggling. He forced himself to smile. "It was great, Mom. Everything went . . . great."

"You held up okay?"

Will nodded. "Uh-huh."

She smiled, and her whole face relaxed. "That's wonderful. Why don't you come outside and tell us about it? Your father will want to hear how everything went."

Will winced. The thought of inching his way through the house and out to the patio was almost more than he could tolerate.

Then an image of Ken Matthews with his arms locked around Melissa sprang into his mind. He grabbed his crutches and started stumping his way toward the backyard. No way was he going to back down. No way.

As far as everybody in his life knew, he was getting better every day. He'd get back on top no matter what.

And then he'd make Ken and Melissa face up to what they'd done.

Jade picked up the low sounds of the television before she even had her key in the lock of her apartment door. *Great.* Her mother was already home. Now she wouldn't get any time at all alone to calm herself down. She stood outside for a second, trying to get her head together before she went in. Her mother was already stressed. Jade didn't want to make her freak out completely by spilling the news about the meeting with Mrs. Delbanco and her problems at work. There wasn't anything her mom could do about it. All it would do was worry her more, which she certainly didn't need right now.

Jade could handle it on her own. She'd just have to.

The minute Jade swung open the door, her mother turned around on the sofa, a surprised look on her face. "I thought you were working until nine," she said.

"I was. I, um . . . I don't feel that good," she said. Which wasn't exactly a lie. She felt terrible.

Her mother's brow instantly creased. "What's wrong?"

Jade walked in and dropped her stuff on the floor, then sat down next to her mom on the sofa. "I just . . . I have a headache," she explained.

Her mother picked up the remote and switched off the TV. She put her hands in her lap and focused her attention on Jade. "Something else is wrong," she said firmly. "What is it?"

Jade opened her mouth to deny it, but tears clogged her throat, making her eyes burn. She drew in a ragged breath, trying to stop the panic from overwhelming her again.

"Jade, tell me what's going on," her mother pressed.

Jade shook her head, unable to speak because of the tightness in her throat.

"Tell me," Ms. Wu repeated. She scooted closer to Jade.

Jade blinked back the tears. "I . . ." She couldn't do it. She couldn't keep all this stress locked inside her anymore. "Okay," she whispered. She twisted her fingers together in her lap. "Mom," she said, "the school social worker called me into her office today." She risked a glance up and saw her mother flinch. "Dad called her this morning and said all this stuff about you—about us. He told her all about wanting

125

to get custody of me, and the social worker said we need to have a meeting with him."

"It's okay. Mrs. Delbanco called me at the bank." Her mother put an arm around Jade's shoulders and squeezed her. "We can handle this."

Jade's breath caught. So her mom already knew? That kind of made sense, actually. Ms. Wu had to come to the meeting, so of course Mrs. Delbanco would have told her about it. Somehow Jade's grip on logic had been slipping lately.

"B-But he's going to make up all these lies," Jade protested. "How are we going to *handle* that?"

"We've gotten through a lot of things together, haven't we?" Ms. Wu asked. Jade nodded. "Then we'll fight this. That's what you want, isn't it?"

"Of course it is," Jade burst out. It was all she wanted.

Her mother smiled gently. "Good. Then we'll fight. I doubt your father could take on both of us and win." She patted Jade's leg, and then she looked Jade straight in the eye, her dark eyes serious. "There isn't anything I wouldn't do to keep you with me, if it's where you really want to be. I want you to know that."

Jade released a deep breath, relieved that her mother was pulling herself together. She grinned at her. "Does that include buying me a new car?" she teased.

126

Her mother laughed. "Don't push it," she said. Then she got up. "I think I need some chocolate ice cream. You want some?"

Jade nodded. "Sure."

She watched as her mom made her way into the kitchen, smiling to herself. Up until tonight she'd been scared that she'd have to go up against her dad alone. But obviously her mom was more ready to stand up for them than she'd realized.

Still, she was just one small woman with no money at all. Jade's father was a slick, sophisticated businessman with tons of money to throw around. What if whatever her mom did wasn't enough?

Jeremy Aames

<u>Reasons</u> Jessica <u>and</u> I <u>Make</u> <u>a</u> <u>Bad</u> <u>Couple</u>

1. Jessica jumps right in the middle of other people's problems. I don't, and I'm not so happy with the types of people she thinks she needs to help.
2. We don't like the same movies or the same music.
3. She's a flirt, and I can get jealous.
4. We make each other mad really easily.
5. She's a great kisser, she's beautiful, she makes me laugh, she gets along with my sisters, she has an incredible heart and doesn't even realize it—

Okay, I'm in deep trouble here.

"Those black platforms definitely work," Cherie told Melissa as she slammed her locker shut.

Melissa smiled down at the black suede shoes, admiring the way her silver toe ring looked with them. "Yeah, they do, don't they?"

"I have to get to calc," Cherie said, flipping her auburn hair over her shoulder. "I'll see you later, 'kay?"

"Yeah, see you later," Melissa responded, already searching the hall behind Cherie for Ken. Normally they met up between classes, but maybe he'd had something he had to do.

Melissa waited by her locker a minute, but there was still no sign of Ken, so she finally started heading for class. She had just rounded the corner when she bumped into someone and stopped, glancing up at the person.

Her heart rate jumped when she recognized Will's face. She quickly took a step back and let her eyes flicker over him, pity welling up inside her. He looked so much smaller and weaker with the crutches propping him up. And he moved so awkwardly. Not at all like the fluid, graceful, confident athlete he used to be.

"Hi," Melissa said.

Will just glared at her, then looked away.

Melissa felt a burst of resentment. She still cared about him—how could he act like she didn't matter? *He* mattered to her more than . . .

More than anyone. Certainly more than Ken ever could.

She blocked out the thoughts, concentrating on coming up with some way to save the situation without letting Will humiliate her.

"So, you're walking pretty well with those," she said, pointing at the crutches.

Will snorted. "Yeah, right."

Melissa fidgeted with her backpack, moving it higher up on her shoulder. "No, you look good. Really."

A muscle twitched in the side of his jaw, and Melissa could see the color rise in his cheeks. "Whatever," he mumbled. "I really could do without the pity compliments, Melissa."

"It's not pity. I just—" Melissa bit her lip in frustration. "I just thought we could be friends."

Ignoring her, Will slid the tips of his crutches ahead of him. "I don't really care what you think," he said, his voice hard. "Don't you get that by now?" He set his crutches ahead of him and started to brush past her.

"But I just want you to be okay," Melissa blurted out, her voice trembling. Instantly she regretted having made herself vulnerable like that. She knew he'd just throw her feelings back in her face.

Will stopped and glanced back at her, balancing on his crutches. "Let me get this straight. You bail out on me when I need you and start dating the guy who couldn't wait to rush in and take my place. And now you think we should be friends? You want me to be okay." He laughed. "That's wonderful."

Melissa had no idea what to say. Yes, her being with Ken probably seemed wrong to him, but couldn't Will see the pain in her eyes? Didn't he know her well enough to understand how badly it hurt her to see him like this?

"But Will, I do care." She took a step forward, but the fire in his expression stopped her from coming closer. "I know how awful this is for you, and I—"

"You have no idea what this is like for me," Will cut her off. His eyes narrowed to tiny slits. "You are the last person I'd want to be friends with. You don't even have a clue how to *be* a friend."

Melissa's hands almost shook from the force of

his words. They'd spent so long together—how could he not see that she truly cared?

Deep inside, a flicker of her own anger sprang up. She was really trying here, and all he was doing was yelling at her.

"You're the one who has no idea how to have a relationship, you know," she shot back.

Will frowned. "Excuse me?"

"Yes, that's right," she said, standing up straighter. "I tried to be there for you. You wouldn't even let me come to visit you in the hospital because I might see you looking like, what, not the perfect jock?" She shook her head. "You're the shallow one here, Will."

Will laughed. "Right, shallow. I don't think I'd go there if I were you." He turned his back on her again. "Whatever gets you ahead, Melissa," he mumbled over his shoulder.

Melissa let out a tiny gasp. He'd never said anything like this to her before. She couldn't believe Will was capable of being so harsh.

"At least I still have a chance to get ahead," she fired back at him as he started making his way down the hall. She paused, then turned and ran in the other direction, pushing her way through the other students.

Normally she'd never let herself be seen like this. But she had to make it to the bathroom, fast, or people would see something worse—they'd see Melissa Fox, queen of cool, in tears.

Jade had her books packed up five minutes before the bell rang at the end of study hall. When it finally did chime, she shot out of the room. If she hurried, she could make it out to her Nissan before anybody else hit the parking lot. Then she could drive home for lunch and spend a few minutes by herself. She'd been trying to stay calm all day, but it wasn't working, and by fourth period her head was so full of panicked thoughts she didn't think she could carry on a normal conversation.

Once she got outside into the crisp sunlight, she felt a little better, like at least some part of her black mood had lifted. She was standing next to her car, fishing her keys out of the bottom of her backpack, when she heard someone calling her name.

She cringed and quickly plastered a fake smile on her face before turning around to see who it was.

The smile melted into a genuine grin. Evan Plummer was heading toward her, waving. Something about the sight of his baggy cargo shorts and thickly woven cotton pullover was more reassuring right now than anything else she could imagine.

"Hi," she greeted him.

"I thought that was you," he said as he approached

her. He flashed a casual grin, then gently tossed his long hair out of his eyes.

Jade felt a slight skip in her chest at the thought that he'd maybe been looking for her. "Yep, it's me," she said.

He pointed to her keys. "Are you in a big hurry?"

"No," she found herself saying. "You?"

Evan bounced up and down on the balls of his feet. "Only to get to lunch. I'm craving those burritos from that taco shack down by the beach. If I hurry, I can make it down there and back before the end of lunch hour. You want to come?"

"No, I—," Jade started to say automatically. But not wanting company right now didn't mean not wanting *Evan's* company. "Sure," she said. "But what if I drive—we'll get there faster."

"Great." Evan hurried around to the passenger side of her car and waited for her to slide in and unlock his door.

"So, how's everything going?" he asked as she steered through the parking lot. "Did Mr. Wakefield have any good advice the other day?"

Jade stared straight ahead, waiting for her turn to exit the lot. "Not really," she admitted.

"Sorry," he said. "Hey, you know, maybe your father won't—"

"He already has," Jade interrupted him. "He

called Mrs. Delbanco and gave her this huge story about how awful my mom is and how I should be living with him." She tried to keep the bitterness out of her voice, but she had a pretty good idea it didn't work.

Evan winced. "Well, there goes that idea."

"Yeah." Jade grabbed the gear lever to shift into third, holding on a little more tightly than necessary.

"Hey," Evan said soothingly. He covered her hand with his warm one. "We just have to think of something, that's all. There's got to be a way to win this."

Jade tried to let his calm, logical presence soothe her, but it wasn't working very well. "It's going to have to be fast," she said. "Mom and I have to have a meeting with Mrs. Delbanco and my father tomorrow. I can't even think about being in the same room with him," she added, her voice rising. "I don't know what I'm going to do."

"Would it help if I came with you?"

Jade glanced over at him. He asked it so simply, so directly. It was mind-blowing. He barely knew her, and he was volunteering to sit through this ultrapersonal meeting just because it might make her feel better.

"If you need moral support, I'd be happy to do it," he repeated. "Not a problem."

Jade loved the way he said that, as if there was no

question he'd do what he said. But she still shook her head. Her mother hadn't even met him, and her dad could probably find some way to twist Evan's presence there into something bad about Jade and Ms. Wu. Besides, Jade had a bad feeling that things would get really ugly in that meeting, and as nice as Evan was, she didn't exactly feel like letting him hear all the insults her father threw around.

She turned the car onto Mission Street and headed downtown. "Thanks anyway, though," she said, giving Evan a grateful smile. "That's sweet. But I don't even know if Mrs. Delbanco would let someone outside of the family be there."

"Yeah, you're probably right," he replied. He traced a finger across the sparkly sticker plastered on the center of her dashboard. "So what are you doing to keep yourself from stressing out while you wait? Are you finding ways to distract yourself?"

"I'm trying." *And it hasn't been working,* she added to herself.

"What about later today? Are you doing anything after school?"

Jade frowned. "No, actually. Cheerleading practice got canceled because Coach Laufeld has a meeting, and I'm not on the schedule at Guido's." That meant a whole afternoon to drive herself crazy worrying about the meeting. Not good.

"You could come to my swim meet," he offered. "It might be better than hanging out by yourself. You know you're just going to drive yourself crazy."

Jade laughed. She couldn't help it. This guy was a serious mind reader. "I probably would," she agreed. "Let's see, cute guys in small bathing suits, right? Yeah, okay, I'll come."

Evan laughed. "That's not exactly how I'd describe my swim meets, but okay. . . ."

Jade glanced at him out of the corner of her eye, noticing that his cheeks were tinged with pink. *Gotcha,* she thought. Evan was so calm and self-assured. He was usually the one doing the teasing—it was fun to turn the tables.

In fact, hanging out with him was really the most fun she'd had in a while. It was too bad he was on that giving-up-dating kick. But now wasn't the greatest time for her anyway. And maybe it wouldn't be too long before something made him change his mind.

"Nice pass, Matthews," Josh Radinsky called out as Ken's throw went sailing about thirty yards past his intended receiver. Next to him Ken heard Matt Wells laugh.

"Yeah, nice pass," Matt muttered. "If you were aiming for dirt."

Ken resisted the urge to turn and sock him. Instead he motioned for the offense to get back into the huddle, then called out the next play. "Handoff to Jake," he told the guys. They broke and headed for their positions. As he took his position behind the offensive line, Ken stared over at the empty bleachers across the field. An image of Melissa in her cheer-leading uniform flashed through his mind, making him smile. He loved watching her cheer, feeling like she was totally behind him.

Still, things were moving pretty fast. It seemed like they'd become this big-time couple in a really short time. She practically had his life planned, and they didn't even know each other that well yet. Maybe he and Maria really hadn't been right for each other, but he wasn't so sure that he and Melissa were either.

And it was hard getting Jessica's words out of his head. What would Olivia think if she had seen him kissing Melissa in the hallway, in front of Will? He cringed at the thought.

Ken shook his head. He had to get his mind back in the game. He lined up behind the center, Brian Cogley, and counted down the snap. "Hike," he yelled, opening his hands for the ball.

Brian handed it back to him. Ken's fingers glided across the smooth surface, but he couldn't get his hands firmly around the ball, and it dribbled back between his legs. Coach Riley blew his whistle. "Dead ball," he yelled.

Ken shut his eyes in frustration. He was playing like a freshman who didn't know what he was doing.

Matt banged into his shoulder as they moved back into the huddle. "Great hands there, Matthews," he mumbled.

Ken tried to ignore him. Getting upset about Will Simmons's friends wasn't going to make him play any better. Besides, that was just what they wanted— to see him fall flat on his face.

Maybe you deserve to. The thought hit him like a blind tackle. What if Jessica was right? Was he being a complete jerk? He sighed, tugging at the strap on his helmet. He needed to concentrate on football. Football. Not his disaster of a social life.

He started running through possible plays in his head. Out of the corner of his eye he saw Coach Riley walk up to the huddle. "Let's can the full-team scrimmages, guys," he said, watching Ken closely. "I want to see some rollout patterns. Matthews, let's see if you can hit the receivers this time."

Ken nodded, swallowing back his embarrassment. He laced his fingers together, cracking his knuckles. Hit the receivers. He could do that. He'd thrown these patterns hundreds of times over the past four years. He'd just concentrate on the ball and what his body needed to do and ignore Simmons's goons.

He wound back his arm and threw, but the pass fell short by at least ten feet. His receiver, Beau Adams, dove for it and just barely came up with the ball.

They lined up to run the play again, and Ken kept his gaze focused on Beau, shutting everyone else out. This time he hit Beau squarely on the numbers.

See, he told himself. *All you have to do is concentrate. Pay attention to what you have to do.*

"Glad you can make the short ones," Radinsky whispered as he moved back into position.

Anger surged through him, squashing the small triumph he'd felt. Ken tried to take slow, deep breaths as he waited for Coach Riley to blow his whistle, signaling the snap. Slow, deep breaths. No anger, no fear.

Brian shot the ball into his hands, and Ken backed up into the pocket and waited, counting off the time until his receiver would be in position downfield. Five seconds, six, seven. He fired. The ball wobbled into the air and sailed right off the field between the goalposts.

"Yeah, Matthews, way to blow it," Matt yelled out.

A couple of the other players snickered.

Coach Riley blew his whistle. "Let's call it on that one for today," he said. The formation immediately disintegrated as everybody headed for the sideline.

Ken stayed where he was in the middle of the field and slowly reached up to unsnap the chin strap on his helmet. He'd had just about enough of Radinsky and Wells. One more word out of either of them and he was ready to pound their heads in.

A shadow crossed the field in front of him. Ken looked up to see Coach Riley standing next to him, his hands on his hips. "Not one of your better days, Matthews," he said.

"No, sir," Ken agreed.

The coach ran a hand across the stubble of beard on his chin. "You can't afford to have bad days anymore, not with Krubowski still waiting to make his decision and the other scouts checking things out. You know that, don't you?"

Ken stared down at his grass-stained cleats. He nodded. "I know. I just—"

"Ken, it doesn't matter what's going on. You've just got to handle it. Now. If you don't, Michigan's going to be offering that scholarship to someone else. Got it?"

Ken glanced over at the other players. They weren't even bothering to hide the fact that they were watching. "I've got it," he mumbled.

"I hope so," Coach Riley said. He turned and walked off.

Ken watched him head toward the other players. Yeah, he got it perfectly. He was blowing it on the field, and he was blowing it in his personal life too.

AREA FOOTBALL STARS VYING FOR COLLEGE TEAMS
By Ed Matthews

Scouting season is here, and colleges and universities from all across the country are seriously considering making scholarship offers to several of our local players. Eager to entice their top choices to sign with them, schools will be making their decisions in the next couple of weeks.

Some of our local standouts include

*Troy Merit of North Arlington. Troy has been the leading rusher in the entire South Coast league for two seasons. In addition, he's a top student who consistently makes honor roll.

*Jeff Page of Big Mesa. Jeff's been an outstanding defensive back for Big Mesa for the past three years, lettering even as a freshman. In addition to his consistent record he's got the size and speed to attract big schools.

*Ken Matthews of Sweet Valley. As quarterback last year, Ken, then a junior, was named league MVP. He got off to a slower start this season, even losing the starting spot. Hopefully he's on his way back up. If the scouts see another excellent season from him this year, they may be willing to overlook a minor glitch in Ken's performance.

These players are only a few of the outstanding talent scouts are seeing in our area. Competition is fierce for full-ride scholarships, and college coaches say they're looking for more than just great statistics. They need to be convinced that a player has the concentration, work ethic, and determination to be consistently great. We at the *Sweet Valley Tribune* would like to wish all our local athletes the best of luck and remind them that only true perseverance will help them make it to the top.

Rebound Girls

9

The starting gun went off to signal the beginning of the swim meet, and Jade jumped slightly. She couldn't remember ever being this nervous. She let out a short breath, then focused on the meet. Evan and the other swimmers dove off their platforms, churning the blue water into a white foam as they headed toward the far side of the pool. Evan's feet left the water as he did a flip turn at the other edge. She cupped her hands around her mouth.

"Go, Evan!" she screamed, although she had no idea if he could hear her or not.

It looked like he was in the lead. Her heart beat faster, just like when the Gladiators needed to score late in the fourth quarter. Who would have guessed swim meets could be so exciting?

"Hey, there."

Jade glanced up and saw Jessica standing next to her. Jessica sank down onto the bleachers, crossing her legs. "What are you doing here?" she asked. "Since when are you a swimming fan?"

145

Jade felt her face get warm. She wasn't sure how Jessica would react to the idea of her and Evan hanging out. "Um, Evan invited me," she said with a shrug.

Jessica's eyes widened. "Really? I didn't realize you guys were friends." She paused, a small smile creeping over her face. "Is there something going on I should know about?" she asked.

"No, of course not," Jade answered quickly.

Jessica's expression didn't change, and Jade could tell she wasn't buying it. "About a week ago you two met for the first time, and now Evan's inviting you to his swim meets, but nothing's going on?" she challenged.

Jade bit her lip. "We kind of ran into each other at the Riot last weekend," she explained. "And he knows about this stuff with my dad . . . he just thought I could use a distraction today, that's all." She paused, frowning. "What about you? How come you're here?" *And not with your boyfriend,* she couldn't help thinking. Did Jessica have to show up around every guy Jade liked?

"Well, since cheerleading practice was canceled, I figured I'd stop by and support Evan," Jessica said. "But you know, I've been to a lot of these before. And I've never seen *you* around . . ."

"Jess, this is nothing, really," Jade insisted. She

shifted, trying to keep her legs from falling asleep. "Evan doesn't even want a relationship," she added. "He made it very clear. He's sick of rebound girls." She caught sight of Evan's toned arms as he surged forward, ahead of his other competitors. She really needed to change the subject, or she'd end up spilling to Jessica how much she was starting to wish Evan *was* up for dating someone—someone very specific.

"What about you and Jeremy?" she asked. "How's that going?" Come to think of it, Jessica hadn't been as annoyingly giddy lately.

Jessica took in a sharp breath. "Not that good, actually. We've been fighting. A ton."

Jade turned to stare at her. "*You guys,* fighting? The super–soul mates? That is definitely not normal."

"No kidding," Jessica said. She twirled a few strands of hair around her finger, inspecting them for split ends. "But we can't seem to get along for five minutes. Everything we talk about ends up getting us into a huge argument." She sighed and brushed her hair back off her shoulder. "You know, I've even been wondering if we—if we belong together."

Jade's eyebrows shot up. After everything the three of them had been through to get Jessica and Jeremy back together, they were already doubting if it was right? How crazy were they?

147

"Okay, reality check," Jade said. "You guys spent months moping around because you weren't with each other. Now you're going to let a couple of stupid fights break you up? You do realize that normal couples fight, don't you?" Jade couldn't help letting a slightly snide tone slip into her voice. It was just so hard to muster pity for a girl who had everything and still couldn't be happy.

Jessica frowned. "Yeah, but not all the time," she mumbled. "I just wish I could believe you're right."

"Right about what?" a deep voice asked from behind them.

Jade spun around, startled. Evan was standing on the bleacher above theirs, drops of water still covering his body—his very exposed body. Jade almost felt like she should look away, but it was hard not to focus on his well-toned chest.

"Did you win?" Jessica blurted out.

"Of course." Evan grinned and shook his head like a wet dog, splattering Jessica and Jade.

"It's a good thing you're cute," Jessica said in a threatening tone.

Evan looked past Jessica to Jade. "Good thing," he repeated, his eyes locked with hers. Jade felt her face getting hot and quickly broke the stare. "Nice of you two to actually pay attention, though," he said. "I thought you came to *watch*."

Jessica shrugged. "We watched," she argued. "We just missed that, um, end part. You know, where you see—"

"Who won," Evan interrupted, grinning. "Anyway, I'm starving. I just need to change, and then I'm heading over to Garden of Eatin' for a snack. Do you want to come?"

Jessica glanced at Jade. "Sounds fine to me," she said. "Are you up for it?"

"Um, sure," Jade answered. She definitely wanted to spend more time around Evan, and the last thing she wanted was to be home, where she'd just obsess about the meeting with her dad. But she couldn't help being disappointed that Evan had asked *both* of them to go. A threesome wasn't even close to a real date. But then again, Evan didn't want to go on a date. He'd told her that.

And all I need to do is change his mind, she thought. She liked challenges—they brought out the best in her. It was something she planned to show Evan, and it was something she hoped her dad would learn soon too.

"That was much more fun than practice," Cherie said as she, Melissa, Amy Sutton, and Gina Cho headed toward the SVH parking lot.

"I kind of missed the workout," Melissa said. When she'd found out that cheerleading practice was canceled today, she had come up with the plan to get her friends to stick around and make spirit posters for the football team. That way she could time it so they were still leaving school right around the same time Ken would get out of practice. She needed a chance to show everyone that she and Ken were the new hot item and stay in control of her image.

Perfect, she thought as she caught sight of Ken walking toward his Trooper.

"Hurry up, you guys," Melissa commanded, hurrying in Ken's direction. "I have to get my CD back from Ken. He's had it for a week."

Even with Cherie trailing along behind them in her three-inch heels, they made it to Ken's car a second before he got there. He looked tired but cute as ever, his blond hair damp from the postpractice shower. She couldn't help flashing back to the way Will used to look after his workouts, when they'd meet up here and he'd drive her home. . . .

"What's up?" Ken asked when he caught sight of her.

Melissa held back a sigh. It wasn't exactly the romantic greeting she'd been hoping for. She immediately pushed Will out of her head and moved closer to Ken, raising herself up on her tiptoes to give him a kiss on the cheek. "Hey, there," she said. "How was practice?"

"It was okay." He didn't move to put his arms

around her or kiss her back, and Melissa stiffened, trying not to let the humiliation affect her.

"Oh," she said, casting a glance back at her friends. They were standing by the back of his car, watching silently. "Well, I just stopped by to pick up that CD you borrowed."

Ken cocked his head. "I don't have any of your CDs."

Melissa pressed her lips together, anger surging up inside her. Didn't Ken know that he should just go with whatever she said in front of her friends? What was his problem? "Yeah, you do," she said firmly. "I had it in the car when we went to the beach that night." She smiled, running her fingers along his arm. "We watched the stars, got close. . . ."

Ken barely reacted. He reached into his backpack to dig around for his car keys. "I don't remember any CD," he muttered.

Melissa took a slow, deep breath. She had to do something fast, before this whole thing blew up in her face. She could just imagine the conversation Gina and Cherie would have later. *Poor Melissa, hung up on a guy who's so obviously not interested.*

She forced a laugh. "I guess I must have lost it somewhere else," she said, hoping she didn't sound too lame. "Anyway, I'll talk to you tonight, okay?"

"Sure," Ken said. He unlocked his door and paused for a second, staring at her expectantly, as if he was waiting for her to just get out of there so he could leave.

"Great," she said in an upbeat tone. She didn't let even a trace of the anger that was building up inside her leak out. "I guess we should go," she said to her friends.

Amy looked at her watch. "I'm supposed to cook tonight. My mom's going to kill me if I don't get home soon."

Melissa looked at Ken, who still stood next to his open door. He was clearly getting ready to drive off without giving her a hug or a kiss or anything. Didn't he have any idea how a boyfriend was supposed to act? Will would never have pulled something like this. Maybe Ken was going to require more work than she'd thought.

"Okay, well, we'd better go," she said, stepping back from Ken. At least it wouldn't look like she was clinging, asking for something he wasn't offering.

Luckily her friends weren't even paying much attention. When she walked over to them, Cherie had taken off her shoes and was bent over, massaging her feet. "We need to get out of here," she said with a moan. "My feet are killing me."

Melissa rolled her eyes. She wished tight shoes were the worst of *her* problems.

*   *   *

Jessica lifted a forkful of soba noodles from the steaming bowl in front of her and stared at them, watching the broth slide down the strands and drip back into the dish.

"Not good?" Evan asked, his brow furrowed.

"Oh, no, it's great," Jessica answered. It wasn't the restaurant's fault she didn't really have an appetite. Still, she didn't want to put a damper on the afternoon for Evan and Jade, so she made herself take a bite.

She looked across the table into Evan's concerned gaze and thought about the last time she'd been at the Garden of Eatin' with him—on their first date.

It seemed like a million years ago. She studied his handsome face, trying to conjure up memories of what she'd felt when she was here with him that night. She'd definitely admired his looks as much as she did now. Evan was gorgeous, when he actually took time to clean himself up. But she could still imagine how amazed she'd been that she could sit across a table from somebody so cute and not have any reaction at all.

No shortness of breath, no tingling, nothing. Not at all like the way she felt when she looked into Jeremy's eyes. At the time she hadn't gotten it. She'd thought maybe she was being shallow, like her friends said. Writing Evan off for not being a super-jock like her usual boyfriends. But finally she'd figured out that a guy could be great looking, sensitive, and even funny, but if he wasn't The One, then none of that mattered.

The sound of Jade's laughter brought Jessica's attention back to the table. Jade was looking at Evan, her expression revealing what a big liar she was for claiming not to be interested in him. "*You're* the one who changed the SV on the hill into a peace sign back in September?" she asked him.

Evan crossed his arms over his chest and sank back against the torn vinyl seat, a satisfied smirk on his face. "Uh-huh. You're not going to get all over my case about not having school spirit, are you?"

Jade just shook her head, smiling. "I thought it was really cool, actually."

Evan's eyebrows rose. Jessica took that to mean Jade had passed the first test.

"Here." Jade pushed a bowl of green pods toward Evan. "You have the last one."

"I can't believe you know what edamame is," Evan said. He scooped the pod out of the bowl and tore it open. He popped the small, green, pealike beans into his mouth and chewed.

Jade rolled her eyes. "You're not the only one who's ever heard of soybeans, Granola Boy."

Evan choked, the mouthful of food apparently stuck halfway down his throat. He reached for his water glass. "Sorry, Miss Food Expert," he said when he could talk again. He grinned at Jade, and she grinned back.

Jessica reached for her melon smoothie and took a big swallow. The electricity between Jade and Evan was obvious. She wondered how long it would take before they noticed.

She and Jeremy had realized what was going on between them pretty fast, even if it had taken forever for them to get together. She'd known right from the beginning that Jeremy was special, and she was pretty sure he'd known it when he met her too. They'd had the sparks that Jessica and Evan had never shared. But it was more than just that energy of attraction. Jessica'd had that with Will, and things with him had turned out to be a total disaster. Jessica and Jeremy *connected*.

But if that was true, then why were things so awful now, when there wasn't anything in their way?

Notes between Maria, Tia, and Jessica
in Drama Class on Wednesday Afternoon

Hey, guys—
   I saw The Dreaded Couple (you know,
K & M) walking into the building this morning,
holding hands (insert barfing noises here). I'm
now officially in need of major retail therapy.
Want to join me at the mall after school?
Jessica, feel free to bag if you have plans with
Jeremy. . . . I'll understand (wink, wink).
                                              —M.

HEY, MARIA—
   HANG IN THERE, GIRL! A GUY
WHO THINKS MELISSA FOX
COULD IN ANY WAY COMPARE TO
YOU? HUGE MORON. REALLY. I
LIKE THE WAY YOU'RE THINKING,
THOUGH. A COUPLE OF NEW
OUTFITS AND HE'LL BE ERASED
FROM YOUR MIND. LET'S DO IT.
                                      —TIA

~~Maria~~

~~Sure, I can go to the mall. I'm not doing anything with Jeremy. Probably not ever again.~~

~~Sure, I can go to the mall. I'm in serious need of retail therapy too. What's the limit on your parents' Gold card?~~

~~Sorry, I can't make it. I'm too busy stressing out about my doomed relationship.~~

Sorry, I can't make it. I've got way too much homework tonight. What about this weekend?

— Jessica

Something to work on

". . . and remember, Wednesdays are two-for-one miniature golf days at the Fantasy Island Fun House. Laser tag, golf, and the latest arcade games from Atari, Sega, and more. Fantasy Island Fun House."

Jessica winced and punched another button on the Jeep's radio, switching off the commercial. She'd spent all day in a terrible mood, obsessing over what to do about things with her and Jeremy. Watching Evan and Jade yesterday had only reminded her of how easy things used to be between them and how much she missed that time.

She stopped at the light on Mission Street and glanced at her bulging backpack on the passenger seat. She'd been so distracted this week that she'd blown off all her homework assignments. Now it was Wednesday, and she had enough work to keep both her and Elizabeth busy for a long time. But she still couldn't even think about looking at any of it.

What she really felt like doing was locking herself

in a room with Jeremy until they worked things out. Or didn't.

She knew that Jade was right about not letting small things get in the way of being happy. But lately it was more like the "happy" moments were interrupting the constant fights. Why couldn't Jeremy handle her worrying about Will? Was he going to be stuck on that forever? She'd managed to get past his relationship with Jade, one of her good friends.

The light turned, and Jessica pressed on the gas. If only she had a magic rewind button. She'd take them back to the beginning of their relationship, when it was easy.

She glanced down at the radio, remembering the idea she'd had on Sunday to try to plan something fun for her and Jeremy. Maybe that commercial for Fantasy Island Fun House was some kind of sign that she should go there. Jeremy wouldn't be with her, but maybe something about the atmosphere there would help jolt her back into why she and Jeremy were right for each other. *And it's not like I'm going to get any homework done anyway,* she thought, giving her backpack another guilty glance. She turned down Beach Street and headed out toward the ocean.

Five minutes later she was right in front of the Fantasy Island Fun House flashing neon sign. The parking lot was almost empty, and even the bike rack outside the front door only held two new-looking mountain bikes. What did she expect? The arcade wasn't exactly an after-school hot spot for kids old enough to drive. Feeling a little silly, Jessica parked the Jeep and went inside.

The shrieking sounds of space guns zapping video aliens hit her immediately, along with the smell of popcorn and nachos. She hesitated just inside the door.

"Awesome shot! This is so much better than Tank Commander."

Jessica turned toward the shout. To her left, a group of junior-high boys were clustered around one of the larger video games, all staring intently at the screen. To her right, more video games lined the walls. Halfway through the room she passed the Doomslayer game. She stopped, staring up at the gaudy graphic of a black-capped monster, his gnarled hands drawn around the scoreboard at the top. She reached out to touch the cold, plastic joystick. In her mind she could see Jeremy's stunned expression when she'd beat him so easily.

Why wasn't he here? If he would have just agreed to come with her on Sunday, she knew he'd be laughing with her right now. It couldn't be that hard to get past their stupid little problems. Not after everything they'd been through.

She shoved her hands in the pockets of her

denim cargo pants. Coming here was having the opposite effect of what she'd hoped. Now all she could think about was how Jeremy had blown her off on Sunday. She didn't want to believe it, but it sure felt like he was blowing off their relationship too.

Jade approached Mrs. Delbanco's office on Wednesday afternoon, pausing just outside the door. She took a deep breath, then reached down to straighten the long, black skirt she'd worn to impress the social worker. Just as she was about to knock, she heard a low murmur from inside, followed by Mrs. Delbanco's loud laugh. She winced, realizing her dad was already in there, charming Mrs. Delbanco.

Jade turned and searched the hall, relaxing when she saw her mother hurrying toward her. "I'm not late, am I?" Ms. Wu asked anxiously when she reached her.

Jade shook her head. "Right on time," she said with a nervous smile.

"Okay, then," Ms. Wu replied. "Let's go in." She lifted her hand and gave a firm knock on the door.

A minute later Mrs. Delbanco opened it. "Ms. Wu, come in," she said. It sounded like she was welcoming dinner guests instead of a mother whose daughter she was trying to take away.

As Jade and her mom followed Mrs. Delbanco into the spacious office used for conferences, Jade spotted her father sitting at the far corner of the table. She couldn't stand to even acknowledge him. Without making eye contact she slipped into a chair at the opposite end and kept her gaze focused on the social worker.

Her mother took the seat next to her, where she could see both Jade's father and Mrs. Delbanco.

Even without looking at her father, Jade could feel his deep frown. The tension in the room was so intense, she wondered how long the air would last.

Mrs. Delbanco stood in front of her seat at the head of the table. "Well, I'm glad you could all make it," she began.

Jade cringed at her soothing tone. As if they would have skipped out on something like this.

Mrs. Delbanco sat down. "I guess we might as well start right in. I thought that since you're the one with concerns, Mr. Wu, I'd have you begin."

Her father sat forward, glancing back and forth between Jade and her mother. "Thank you," he said. "Contrary to what Jade might believe, I've given this situation a great deal of thought. I realize I've been out of touch with her life for some time now, but after seeing the way she's living, I believe I can offer her some important things that her mother can't give her. Things she needs before becoming an adult, on her own."

Mrs. Delbanco nodded, her expression neutral. "I see. For instance?"

Mr. Wu frowned. "For one thing, I've been married for almost ten years. If she were to live with me, Jade would benefit from having two parents in the home—"

Jade bolted forward in her seat. "Susan's not my—"

Before she could finish, her mother laid a hand on her arm, stopping her. Jade closed her mouth and glared at her father.

"As I was saying," he went on, "she'd get a great deal more supervision in my care. Judging from what I hear of her grades, she obviously needs it. And then there's college to consider. Both my wife and I have degrees. We're very committed to helping Jade get into a good school. With her record so far, it's going to take a lot of work, but we're willing to put in the time and effort. Her future is much too important to let slip away."

Jade noticed that Mrs. Delbanco was nodding with each point her father made. Her stomach turned over. She grabbed the edge of the table with her fingers to keep her hands from shaking.

He sounded good. Really good. How could her mother fight against those kinds of arguments?

Ms. Wu sat forward, as if hearing Jade's thoughts. "Excuse me," she said, looking at Mrs. Delbanco. "May I ask a few questions?"

The social worker nodded. "Of course."

Ms. Wu flashed a brief smile. "What about cheerleading?" she asked Jade's father. "If Jade changes schools, she won't be eligible for the rest of the year."

Jade's father shifted in his seat. "Cheerleading? How is that relevant?"

Jade smirked. It was only one of the biggest parts of her life. Of course her dad was clueless about it.

"Well, it's very important to Jade," her mother said. "She's been on the squad for three years, and they've qualified for a regional competition. I can't imagine pulling her out in her senior year would be good for her."

Jade glanced at her father. He was frowning again, his brow wrinkled in concentration.

Ms. Wu turned slightly to face the social worker. "Cheering has been one of the best aspects of Jade's high-school life," she explained. "It's given her incentive to keep her grade average at a B level. What will happen if that's taken away?" She glanced at Jade, smiling. "I don't know how well you know my daughter, Mrs. Delbanco, but Jade's very stubborn. If she decides she's not going to work in school, there's nothing her father or his degrees will be able to do about it."

Go, Mom, Jade thought, mentally pumping her fist in the air.

"And what about her friends?" her mother continued. "Changing schools in the middle of her senior year is going to destroy a lot of friendships. She'll be starting all over with kids who are getting ready to graduate themselves."

"Yes," Mr. Wu cut in, "what about her friends? After seeing her this weekend, I'm under the impression she could use some better influences."

Jade's mother looked at her father. "Really? Which of Jade's friends have you met?" she asked.

"I—" He cleared his throat. "I only met that one boy, but judging from her behavior, I—"

"What behavior? Her cheerleading awards? Her excellent attendance?" her mother prodded. "What exactly has she done that's so bad?"

"She's . . . she's got that . . . that ring in her stomach," he finally spat out.

Jade snickered. Her mother and Mrs. Delbanco were both smiling. Seeing that loosened the tight band of panic squeezing her chest.

"You talked about college, David." Ms. Wu put her arms on the table and leaned forward. "Do you know what she wants to do with her life? What she'd like to study? Do you even know where she works?"

The worry lines that had appeared on his face as her mother started talking were slowly deepening, and Jade felt lighter and lighter.

"We haven't talked about that. No," he admitted.

Jade's mother smiled. "I see. Don't you think it's important to know what her interests are before you think about which colleges to steer her toward?"

"Well, of course it is," he snapped.

Ms. Wu looked at the social worker. "I'm just trying to point out here that while my ex-husband means well, I think, he hasn't spent any time with Jade in the past several years. He may believe he knows what she needs, but he doesn't really know her at all."

Mrs. Delbanco nodded thoughtfully. She turned toward Jade. "I imagine you must have a few things to say."

Jade took a deep breath. "I do." She cleared her throat. For the first time she dared to look her father right in the eye. "I want to say that my mother is great. The best. You have no idea what we've had to go through since you left." She stared him down until his gaze slid away. "My mom has worked herself sick taking care of me, making sure I had everything I needed. She's been there for me my entire life, and I know she always will be. No matter what you try to do, you'll never change that."

Her father looked back and forth from Jade to her mother. Jade could tell he was shocked to hear her defend her mother so strongly.

"But Jade," he protested, "I got the impression you're on your own all the time. I assumed you and your mother weren't that close."

Jade's mouth tightened in anger. "Maybe you should get to know me before you decide things like that."

Her father sighed and rubbed a hand across his eyes. "I'm just worried about your future, that's all."

She smiled at her mother. "I'm happy. There's nothing to worry about."

Her father's shoulders slumped. He nodded. "Okay," he said. "I think I get this. Nothing is quite what it appeared from my visit." He paused, fixing Jade with a pleading gaze. "Try to understand, Jade," he said. "I came to visit, and I saw a daughter with a mother who never seemed to be around. You told me she'd been sick, that she was always working. It looked to me like you were heading for trouble." He sighed and glanced at Jade's mother. "Maybe I was wrong. But I still want you to know that you have another option if you ever want it. I was afraid you felt like I didn't want you in my life, and that's not the case."

Jade sat very still, holding her breath. Was he telling them he was going to back down?

Mrs. Delbanco cleared her throat. "What are you saying, Mr. Wu? Are you changing your mind about the suit for custody?"

Mr. Wu stroked his wide brown tie, smoothing the shiny fabric. "I'm saying I may not have seen the entire picture here." He stopped and looked her mother in the eye. "I'll drop the custody suit if you'll agree to let me visit more often," he said.

Jade bit her lip to keep from yelling. He'd backed down. They'd won!

"David, I've never kept you and Jade apart," Ms. Wu insisted. "How often you visit is between you and Jade. And if you'd like, I can give you more frequent updates on how she's preparing for college. But that really is up to Jade."

Mr. Wu nodded. He turned his gaze to Jade, and she stared back at him directly without flinching. "I think one thing I've realized this week is what I've been missing," he said solemnly. "Maybe that's something we could work on together."

Jade was shocked to realize there were tears collecting in her eyes. She blinked them back, trying to think of how to answer him. She was still so angry that he had done all of this, but the idea that he really did care about her more than she'd thought was making her feel something she'd stopped wishing for years ago—something she hadn't realized how badly she needed.

"Okay," she said softly. "We can work on that."

* * *

Jeremy rubbed a hand through his damp hair, then climbed into his car and slammed the door shut. He was exhausted. Football practice had gone great today, but it had totally wiped him out. Still, it wasn't the workout that had him in such a bad mood. It was this thing with Jessica.

He turned the key in the ignition, and Debbie started right up. He nodded in satisfaction. At least one female in his life was reliable. A line of cars waited to get out of the school lot, and Jeremy maneuvered the Mercedes into the stream and waited his turn, the engine idling smoothly.

He wasn't sure if it was a good thing or not that he and Jessica wouldn't be working together this afternoon. They hadn't talked since their fight on Monday at work. Maybe seeing her would make him realize that things had gotten blown out of proportion, and they were fine. Or maybe they'd just get into another fight and say even meaner stuff than they already had to each other.

What if Jessica's not the person I thought she was? The thought made him wince. He'd been so certain of who she was and what he felt for her. But what if it had all been about them wanting each other to be people they weren't? A big mistake?

The cars in front of him moved, and he turned out onto the street and headed toward home, his head whirling with confusion. He'd gone back and forth, arguing with himself all week, until the whole thing was so tangled in his brain, it didn't even make sense anymore.

For some reason when he reached the turn to his house, he skipped it and kept going. He needed to be somewhere else right now—not home. He turned on the radio and flipped through the stations, cruising down the streets that led toward the ocean. He turned the corner onto Isabelle Street and caught sight of the Fantasy Island Fun House on the left. He slowed down, staring at the entrance. Was this where he'd been heading all along? The place where he and Jessica had first connected?

He parked on the street and turned off the engine, considering whether or not to go inside. Maybe a few games of Doomslayer would clear his head. Yeah, an hour with nothing to do but zap aliens might be just what he needed. It was worth a try anyway.

He shrugged and got out of the car, then hurried inside the arcade. He headed in the right direction, straight for the Doomslayer machine. He'd taken only a couple of steps when he heard the deep, booming, evil laugh coming from the Doomslayer game. Somebody was already playing it. *Sure,* he thought, glancing around the nearly empty arcade. *There are all of five kids in here, and somebody's playing my game.* He sighed and kept going. Hopefully it was some little kid who'd get bored quickly and move on. He stepped around the big motorcycle simulator in the row in front of it, and saw . . .

Jessica?

Before he could say anything, she glanced up, then jerked back in surprise, taking her hands off the controls. "Jeremy?"

He nodded. "Hi."

The game let out a loud, screeching sound to in-dicate that Jessica had just been killed, and her eyes flickered over to the machine, then back to Jeremy. She smoothed a hand over her hair. "Um, what—what are you doing here?"

He smiled. "I don't know. I was driving by and . . ." He stopped, then shrugged. "I just thought I'd come in and play a few rounds of Doomslayer."

Jessica grinned at him. "Yeah," she said. "Me too."

Jeremy leaned back against another game and crossed his legs at the ankles. He suddenly felt better than he had in days. "So, this brings back memories," he said, nodding at the game behind her.

"Yeah, it does," she said, her voice sounding wistful.

Jeremy crossed over and examined the score flashing across the video game's screen. "Looks like you've been practicing," he commented.

Jessica shrugged. "Only one game."

"Think you can still take me?"

Jessica laughed. "Oh, I think so."

Jeremy raised his eyebrows. He fished in his pocket for quarters. "Okay, then," he said, pulling out a few coins. He moved up to the machine until they were standing shoulder to shoulder. He fed the quarters into the machine and held his finger over the start button. "Ready?"

Jessica giggled and pushed his hand down on the button. "Go!" she yelled.

They grabbed their joysticks at the same instant and started firing. They fought hard, each intent on annihilating the mutants that jumped onto the screen. The game wound down with a deep, creepy laugh.

"Shoot," Jeremy whispered when he saw the final score.

"You owe me," Jessica gloated. "I feel the need for nachos."

Jeremy shook his head in mock defeat. "I just can't stand losing to a girl," he mumbled.

Jessica nudged him with her shoulder. "Get over it," she said, laughing. "Come on, I'm really hungry."

They wandered down through the booths toward the concession stand. "I still have that pink pig," Jessica said, pointing to the small, plush toys lined up above the Skee Ball games.

Jeremy laughed. "Yeah, it only cost about eighty-seven dollars by the time I was done." He reached for her hand and felt her shiver slightly at his touch.

He grinned down at her, and she smiled back, her blue-green eyes sparkling in a way he hadn't seen lately.

"You know—," they both started at almost the same time. They stopped, laughing.

"Me first," Jessica said before Jeremy could get out another word. She squeezed his hand. "I've been thinking a lot about what's been happening," she said. "I know I've been overreacting to things." She glanced down at the floor, then back at him. "I just wanted this to work out so badly, I think I panicked when everything wasn't perfect. But so what if we don't always like the same movies?"

"Yeah, next time we can go see something neither of us likes," he teased. He smiled shyly. "That could make for interesting possibilities," he added.

Jessica let out a short laugh and swatted him with her free hand.

Jeremy grabbed her fingers and pulled her toward him, not even caring that they were standing in the middle of the arcade. He put his hands on her shoulders and looked her in the eye. "I think we've both been thinking about this way too much," he said.

"I know," Jessica agreed. "So what do we do?"

Jeremy thought for a second. Then he grinned. "Get nachos and play another round of Doomslayer?" he suggested.

Jessica pulled back, frowning. Then her expression relaxed back into a smile and she came up on her tiptoes to give him a light kiss on the cheek. "Double or nothing?" she whispered into his ear.

A shudder ran through him, and he had to resist the urge to grab her and kiss her right there. He took a deep breath. "I can handle that." Yeah, he could handle losing a hundred games in a row if they could laugh like that together. Okay, maybe not a hundred. He did have his pride.

"Come on, Will, five more of these," Dr. Goldstein, Will's physical therapist, urged as he tried to lift his trembling leg six inches off the floor.

One . . . two. He collapsed back on the floor mat, groaning in pain, and rubbed the tight muscle in the front of his thigh. He couldn't make it.

"That's okay," Colleen said quickly. "We've done enough of those." She knelt next to him and put her hands on his leg just above the cast. "Wow," she said, her voice heavy with concern. "These muscles are tight."

Will screwed his eyes shut, trying to block out the pain while she massaged his trembling muscles. Slowly, carefully, she lifted his leg and moved it back and forth, testing the feel of the ligaments around his knee.

Then she gently laid his leg out straight and frowned down at him. "You've been overdoing it,

Will. These ligaments are inflamed, and your thigh muscle is severely strained."

She straightened up and put her hands on her hips. "You're going to have to back off, give yourself more time to heal. If you don't, you could make it a lot worse, maybe even jeopardize your recovery."

Will sat up. "I'm just a little tired today," he said, brushing off her comments. What did she know anyway? "You said you've never seen anybody come back from this kind of surgery so quickly." He massaged the scar running down the outside of his leg. "I know with my conditioning, I'll be back playing football in no time," he added without thinking.

He froze, realizing what he'd done. He'd told himself he would keep his plans a secret from everyone who didn't believe in him until he knew he was ready. He glanced up at Dr. Goldstein's face, checking for a reaction. He could already anticipate the lecture he'd get about taking things easy, going slow, and all the rest of that meaningless junk.

But Dr. Goldstein didn't have that tense expression she usually got before a warning speech. Instead her eyes were filled with . . . pity. Pity that somehow made Will's whole body go cold.

She knelt back down next to Will and put a hand on his shoulder. "Will," she began, her voice unbearably soft, "I didn't know you were still thinking about football." She paused, swallowing. "I thought you'd been told by now. I—I don't know what to say."

"Just say it," Will told her through clenched teeth. His voice came out flat and hard, and Dr. Goldstein flinched. Then she nodded.

"Okay," she said. "Will, there's no way anybody could play football again after an injury like this. Your knee would never take it, even when it's completely healed."

Will jerked his shoulder out from under her hand. Her words echoed in his head like a prison sentence.

"Didn't your surgeon tell you that?" she asked him.

Will could barely breathe, but somehow he forced out an answer. "He said that, after the surgery," he admitted. He closed his eyes, remembering waking up in that hospital room and hearing Melissa tell him the doctor's verdict. "But I've made all this progress and—" He stopped, choking back the thickness in his throat. "I thought I could prove him wrong," he finished.

Dr. Goldstein sighed. "I'm sorry, Will. You have recovered more quickly than usual for this type of injury, and you'll be able to do a lot of things you can't now. But you had a very severe tear, and I can't see a way that your body could tolerate such a demanding sport ever again."

Will rolled on his side and pushed himself up. The icy sensation he'd felt moments ago had been replaced by a burning heat that surged through his limbs. His useless limbs. He had to get out of here. Now. The only reason he'd put up with all of these torture sessions was to get back out on the football field—and now she was telling him it wouldn't happen. Telling him his future was empty.

His breath came in short, sharp gasps. He groped for his crutches and stuck them under his arms. Without another word to Dr. Goldstein, he turned and limped his way out of the therapy room, relieved that she didn't try to stop him. By the time he made it down the hall and through the reception area to the front door, the rage inside him was overwhelming.

In seconds his whole life had been ripped away from him. Everything that mattered—football, his career, Melissa—it was all gone.

No, not just gone, he realized. *Stolen. Stolen—and delivered right to Ken Matthews.* Ken had everything that Will had lost. There was no way that Will could get any of it back, but maybe it would be enough just to make sure that Ken couldn't keep it either.

JADE WU

8:30 P.M.

Okay, I can start breathing again. It's going to be fine. Even the visits should be okay. I mean, I guess I can put up with my father a couple of times a year.

So now that I don't have to worry about losing my mom, it's definitely time to focus on another part of my life that's been seriously lacking lately. Let's just say I hope Evan's ready to put his little no-girlfriend policy to the test.

KEN MATTHEWS

8:36 P.M.

I need to focus. I need to get my head back in the game and throw better tomorrow, or this is all over. And I really need to do something about this Melissa thing before it gets completely out of control. If it isn't there already.

MELISSA FOX

8:37 P.M.

Something's changed with me and Ken. I can feel it, and I don't know what to do. I have to get him to focus on me again, to remember what matters. I've lost Will. Ken's all I have left—and there's no way I'm letting go of him too.

WILL SIMMONS

8:59 P.M.

Revenge is a lot like getting ready for a big game, right? Know your strengths. Know your opponent's weaknesses. Be ready to battle it out. Keep your focus.

And I'll probably have it easy anyway. I already know that Matthews is a quitter. All I have to do is find a way to bring that back out—and show the team, the coach, and Melissa what my replacement is really made of.